Boys Beware

Boys Beware

JEAN URE

Illustrated by Karen Donnelly

HarperCollins *Children's Books*

For Zahra, and for Tara

First published in Great Britain by HarperCollins *Children's Books* in 2005
HarperCollins *Children's Books* is a division of HarperCollins*Publishers* Ltd,
77-85 Fulham Palace Road, Hammersmith, London W6 8JB

The HarperCollins website address is
www.harpercollins.co.uk

Text © Jean Ure 2005 .
Illustrations © Karen Donnelly 2005

The author and illustrator assert the moral right to be
identified as the author and illustrator of this work.

ISBN-13   978 0 00 716138 6

Find out more about HarperCollins and the environment at
www.harpercollins.co.uk/green

The Beginning

"I wouldn't want you having boys up there," said Mum.

"*Boys?*" I shot a sideways glance at Tash, out of the corner of my eye. Tash shot one back at me. We managed – just – to stifle our giggles. "Mum!" I said. "As if we would!"

"As if you would," said Mum.

"*I* wouldn't," said Ali.

"I'm not worried about you," said Mum. "I'm worried about those two."

This time we couldn't help it. I clapped a hand to my mouth to stifle the squeaks. Tash buried her face in one

of the sofa cushions. The fact is, me and Tash are into boys in a BIG WAY. It is just something that seems to come naturally to us. We look at a boy and we go all gooey, like *oo-er*, mushy peas and soft ice cream, and help, help! I'm going into meltdown! Only if the boy is worth it, of course; we are not indiscriminate! Even at twelve years old, when we were just getting started, we knew better than to go for geeks or cavemen. Mum's problem was that she didn't think we were old enough to get started at all.

"We sent you to the Gables expressly to avoid all that!"

Poor Mum. Poor Dad. Did they really think that shutting us up in a nunnery – well, an all-girls' school, which amounts to the same thing – would keep us safely playing with our dolls till the age of sixteen? *Eighteen,* if Dad had his way. Even older. He's worse than Mum! He once told us that he wished we could remain his little girls for ever. Pur-lease! Yuck yuck double yuck.

It is amazing how naïve parents can be. It never seems to occur to them that even at an all-girls' school there are sometimes men teachers. Some of them quite young and fanciable! Or that girls have brothers. Likewise cousins, *of the male persuasion.* Not to mention a life outside of school.

"It's all very well you smirking," said Mum, "but we all know what would happen… The minute my back was turned you'd start having orgies."

"Orgies!" A series of ecstatic squeaks came bursting out of me. Strange glugging sounds shook the sofa cushion.

"Don't deny it," said Mum. "I've heard of teenage parties getting out of control. You'd start by inviting a handful of friends and end up with hundreds of total strangers, wrecking the place."

The sofa cushion erupted. I got as far as, "Mu-u-u-m—" and then collapsed.

"No, I'm sorry," said Mum. "It really is quite out of the question."

"But, *Mu-u-u-m*—"

"I'd never have a moment's peace, and nor would Auntie Jay. It's not fair to ask it of her."

"We didn't ask it," I said. "She *offered.*"

"Yes, but she didn't realise what she'd be taking on. She doesn't know what it's like," said Mum, "having you lot in the house."

"But we wouldn't *be* in the house! Not her bit of the house. We'd be upstairs, all hidden away... we'd be quiet as mice! She wouldn't even know we were there."

"Yes, and I shudder to think what you'd get up to," said Mum. "You're too young, I'd have nightmares. It's no good, you're not going to talk me round. I shall have to say no."

"Mum, you can't!" Tash suddenly sprang into action, clutching her cushion. "This is your big chance!"

Well! If Tash had decided to enter the fray, I obviously had to support her. Earnestly, I said, "Tash's right, you can't let motherhood ruin your career."

Mum pretended to be amused by this – "It's not going to ruin my career!" – but I could sense that she was wavering. Yippee! We had struck the right note!

"You'd be mad to miss an opportunity like this," I said.

"Yes, and we'd be the ones that paid for it," said Tash. "You'd go round telling people it was our fault."

"Like, all because of us you had to let your big chance slip away from you."

"Which is why you'd ended up as an unfulfilled woman – all mean and bitter and twisted."

Mum said that she would be even more mean and bitter and twisted if she came back home to find we'd given Auntie Jay a nervous breakdown.

I stared at her, reproachfully. "It doesn't say much for the way you've brought us up if that's how you think we'd behave."

"Good try," said Mum. "But the answer is still no!"

She was doing her best to sound like she really meant it. Like that was definitely the last word. End of subject. Finish. But I'd heard Mum on the phone to Auntie Jay and I *knew* how much this job meant to her. Dad is always the one in our family that gets to go away on interesting assignments.  Partly this is because he's a man, and men tend to take it for granted that it's OK for them to go whizzing off across the globe at a moment's notice but not OK for women, at any rate that's how it seems to me. But mainly, I have to say, it's because of his work. Dad is not at all a caveman type; he doesn't expect Mum to stay home washing his socks and ironing his shirts while he's off gallivanting. He does, however, happen to be an archaeologist (hooray! I've remembered how to spell it) and he is very much dedicated to digging things up. Sometimes he digs in this country, but on the whole there is more stuff waiting to be dug up in other parts of the world. Like right

now, for instance, he was out in Peru digging up graves. And Mum had been offered a commission to go and join him, to take pictures for a book. Really exciting! Mum is a brilliant photographer, she is wasted just doing pictures of bouncing babies and giant cucumbers for the local paper. We all thought that she deserved a break. We also thought that it would be pretty cool to spend eight whole weeks living on our own…

I might as well admit it, we weren't just thinking of Mum! Well, me and Tash weren't. I don't know what Ali was thinking. Nobody ever knows what Ali is thinking. Stuff goes on inside her head that has absolutely no relationship whatsoever to the things that are going on around her. Like now. She'd been perched on the arm of a chair, chewing her fingernails (a disgusting habit which she ought to have grown out of years ago) when suddenly she stopped chewing and said, "I'm nearly at the end of *The Next Generation.*"

It sort of made sense, if you happened to know that she is a massive fan of *Star Trek.* It didn't actually seem to have anything to do with what we'd been discussing, but that's Ali for you.

"I'll be moving on to *Deep Space Nine* in a few days."

"Ali, you're not *helping*," said Tash. She turned, to renew the attack on Mum. "Mum, you can't do this to us!"

"Do what?" said Mum.

"Make us the excuse for not getting on with your life! It isn't fair," said Tash. "How do you think it makes us feel?"

"It makes us feel *terrible*," I said.

"It makes us feel *guilty*."

"All those times you've come home grumbling cos of having to do another baby—"

"And now you could be out there doing graves!"

"Tombs," I said, "actually."

"All right, then, tombs."

"*Old* tombs."

"*Ancient* tombs."

"It's got to be better than babies!"

"And just think, you'd get to see your name in print—"

"*Photographs by Catherine Love.*"

"It's what you've always dreamed of!"

Mum bit her lip. We were really starting to get to her!

"I wish you wouldn't," she said. "You're only making it more difficult for me."

"We want to make it difficult!"

"We want to be able to boast about you!"

"Our mum, the famous photographer…"

"Taking photographs out in Peru!"

"But you're too young," wailed Mum. "You're only twelve years old!"

"Mum we're nearly thirteen!"

"Ali's nearly *fourteen*."

The sound of her name brought Ali back to life.

"If we go," she said, solemnly, "I'd have to take them with me."

We all stopped and looked at her. Take what? Take who? Me? Tash?

"My *Deep Space Nine*s."

The penny dropped. For once, I'd actually managed to follow her thought process. Of course! She couldn't possibly be expected to go to Auntie Jay's without her supply of *Star Trek*s.

"Oh, Ali, for goodness' sake," said Mum. "You have a one-track mind!"

"One *trek*," said Tash.

Rather clever, I thought.

"There'd be enough to keep me going," said Ali, "so long as it was only a couple of months – though I suppose I could always come back and get more. If I ran out, I mean. If you decided to stay in Peru for longer than a couple of months."

"Ali, I am not going to Peru," said Mum. But she really didn't say it with that much conviction. I think I knew, then, that we had won!

Two days later, it was all arranged. Mum was going to Peru, and we were going to Auntie Jay's. Hurrah! We were so excited. Mum still had her doubts, but Dad, fortunately, was so busy with his digging, and so eager for Mum to go and take photographs, that he forgot we were his little helpless girls and told Mum that of course we'd be all right.

"Jay will keep an eye on them." He even added that a bit of independence might be good for us. "Teach them a bit of responsibility."

Wonders will never cease!!!

That weekend, me and Mum and Tash went to "view the apartment", as they say. Ali was off somewhere with Louise Wagstaffe, her best friend from school. They are thick as thieves! Mum said, "Why not bring Louise with you?" but Ali said they had things to do. I don't know how she could bear to miss out on all the fun. I mean, a place of our own! There was so much to talk about, so much to decide, like for instance who was going to sleep where, but Ali is the sort of person who really doesn't care about her surroundings. I sometimes think she doesn't even notice them, just so long as she has her beloved *Star Trek*s.

Auntie Jay only lives on the other side of town, so the great advantage, from Mum and Dad's point of view, was that we'd be OK for school. We'd only just started back for the summer term, and they are incredibly strict about not letting us miss any.

"Just remember – " it is their constant cry " – we're paying for you to go to that school!"

Yeah yeah yeah. They have to get their money's worth, I do see that. Me and Tash wouldn't have minded going off to Peru with them. Stuff school! Ali would probably have got fussed, though. She is quite a boffin, in her own peculiar way.

If Ali is a boffin, then Auntie Jay (who is Mum's little sister) is your actual auntie from heaven. She is bliss! What other auntie would have offered the whole top floor of her house to three girls?

Once upon a time, Auntie Jay was "into property". She used to buy it and sell it and make simply oodles of dosh, until after a bit she decided that just making money was rather ignoble, and also not terribly interesting, so she gave it all up and started to work for  herself, instead. She runs this perfume company called *Scents & Flowers*, which advertises on the Internet but is actually located in her basement at home. *Scents & Flowers* doesn't make very much money, but is very rewarding in all kinds of other ways. It does mean, however, that she has to let out most of her house as flats, keeping only the bottom bit for herself. It is lucky that it's quite a large house, bought in the days when she was into property. It is also very old, being built in the year 1905. Which makes it, I think, Edwardian.

So we were going to inhabit the top floor. All by ourselves! Mum said we were extremely lucky that the flat was available. The last tenants had just moved out; we could see where they'd spilled stuff on the carpet and hung things on the wall.

"It really needs redecorating," said Auntie Jay.

But Mum gave one of her hollow laughs, like ha ha you have to be joking, and said, "Wait till this lot have been in here a couple of weeks!"

"Mum, we'll treat it like Buckingham Palace," I said. "I promise!"

"Just don't set fire to anything," begged Auntie Jay, "that's all I ask. Now, let's take you on a guided tour."

The main room, which was like a bedroom and sitting room all in one, was huge. It had a tiny little kitchen opening off it at one end, and an even tinier little bathroom at the other, plus a sort of broom cupboard with just enough space for a bed.

"I thought Ali could have that," said Auntie Jay, "seeing as she's the oldest. I'm afraid you two will have to share. Is that all right?"

There was just the one bed in the sitting room. It was a biggish sort of bed, but we'd never actually had to sleep together before.

"Blimey," said Tash.

"You'd better not kick," I said.

"You'd better not snore!"

Auntie Jay was beginning to look a bit flustered. "Maybe I ought to see if I can find another one somewhere."

"Oh, don't worry about those two," said Mum. "They can make do. They're practically joined at the hip, anyway."

It's true, me and Tash are the hugest of best friends. Mum says we are more like twins than sisters. Sometimes we pretend that we *are* twins, and then people just get so confused! You can see them looking from me to Tash and back again to me, not knowing what to believe. We happen to have been born on *exactly the same day* – yet we don't look in the least bit  alike. Tash is small and dark and elfin, with this dear little face, all beaming and full of innocence. (Totally misleading! Mum says she is a holy terror.) I am on the skinny side, with blonde hair, a bit straggly except when it has just been washed, and blue eyes. In my last school photo, although I say it myself, I looked positively angelic! This is also misleading, according to 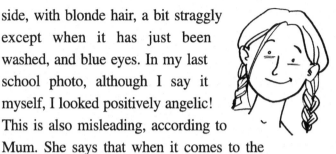 Mum. She says that when it comes to the holy terror stakes, "I couldn't put a pin between you." But physically we are completely and utterly different, and this is because we are actually *not even sisters*! We love to string people along and get them all wound up. And then, when we have teased them long enough, we put them out of their misery. We have this party piece that we do.

"Her *mum* – " Tash says.

"Married her *dad*," I say.

"Which means – " (both together) " – we're not even related!"

Ha ha! Well, we think it's funny. Sometimes we tell people the story of how Mum and Dad met up while me and Tash were still in Infants. We tell how they got talking while they waited for us outside the school gates.

How Mum was on her own with me and Ali, Dad was on his own with Tash, and so in the end they decided to get married. How us three were bridesmaids, in little pink frocks. Just so-o-o sweet!
Yes, and it would have been even sweeter if Ali hadn't gone and brought up her breakfast in the middle of the ceremony, though at least she managed to catch most of it in her bouquet, which Auntie Jay said showed great presence of mind. Personally I thought it was rather disgusting, but it is the sort of thing you expect from Ali. She is just *so* accident prone!

After we'd settled the question of beds, and had mastered the art of switching the cooker on and off and closing the fridge door properly – Mum seemed to think we needed lessons! She has such a poor opinion of us – we all went downstairs for a cup of tea. One of Auntie Jay's friends was there, a woman called Jo Dainty, who used to be at uni with her. She said, "Well, I just hope you're more capable than I was at your age… I couldn't even boil an egg!"

"I can boil *eggs*," I said. I didn't mean to sound boastful but there are times when grown-ups really do seem to think we are quite useless. I mean, closing fridge doors, for goodness' sake!

"Just don't get too cocky," said Mum. "This is going to be a steep learning curve."

She added that she intended to make out a list of Dos and Don'ts, and she advised Auntie Jay to do the same.

"I may even make a Book of Rules."

She thought better of that idea, thank goodness! But the day she moved us into the flat she presented me and Tash with a couple of jotter pads and said she wanted us to keep a daily Food Diary and a weekly Activities Diary, so that when she got back she would be able to check a) what we had been eating and b) what we had been up to.

"Mum!" I said. "That's spying!"

"It's not spying," said Mum. "It's a way of keeping you focused."

"So who gets to do what?" said Tash.

I said that I would do Activities, and she could do Food. Writing a diary was no problem for me, I already kept one anyway. Not that I would ever let Mum see my own personal diary! My personal diary is *strictly private.* I thought that for Mum it would be easy enough just to do extracts. Suitable ones, of course!

"What about Ali? What's she going to do?"

Mum said that Ali was to be responsible for Fat Man. Fat Man is our cat. He is not really fat, it's just that he

has masses of fur, all puffed out like a big pompom, plus *the* most disagreeable expression, which in fact is every bit as misleading as Tash looking innocent and me looking angelic. In reality he is the sweetest cat and we all love him to bits! But it is Ali who specially dotes on him, so we didn't mind her being put in charge. In any case, she would never have managed to keep a diary, she is far too disorganised. Unless, perhaps, she could have put it on the computer. Ali loves her computer! Needless to say, it was going to come with us. The computer and

Star Trek are the two biggest things in her life – well, plus Fat Man.

Some people think that Ali is a bit odd, but really she's just eccentric. We all feel very protective towards her. Dad once said that she is your actual "innocent abroad", by which I think he meant that she is not at all streetwise. Unlike me and Tash! I wasn't altogether surprised when Mum took me to one side, as we loaded the car for the second trip to Auntie Jay's, and said, "Emily, I want you and Tash to do something for me... I want you to watch out for Ali. Make sure she's all right. I know she's older than you, but she is such a dreamer! So can I rely on you?"

I solemnly gave her my promise. Of course we would watch out for Ali! It made me feel good that Mum trusted me.

Or did she??? The last words she said, as we kissed her goodbye, were: "Just remember... *no boys*. I mean that, you two! I'm serious."

PERSONAL PRIVATE DIARY (not to be confused with Mum's!)
Week 1, Saturday
Our first day of independent living! Not that it has been all that independent so far as it was half-past two when Mum left and at seven o'clock Auntie Jay invited us down to have dinner with her and her friend Jo, so we only had just a few hours on our own. But that was enough to convince us that it is going to be the hugest fun!

Me and Tash started off by moving all the furniture about. It was Tash's idea. She said the way you arrange your living space is an expression of your personality, and it was the other people, the people who had been there before us, who had put the bed in the corner and pushed the table against the wall. She insisted that the bed had to go under the windows, and the table had to go in the middle.

"That way, it'll cover up the stain on the carpet."

I do hope she isn't going to become house-proud! She was actually talking of finding a *rug* to stand the table on. I had to remind her that we are only here for eight weeks. Tash said, "Yes, but we want the place to look nice."

So long as she is not going to nag. I mean, there are more important things to worry about than stains on the carpet. Ali, of course, hasn't even noticed the stain, she spent the entire afternoon sorting out her *Star Trek*s. She has stacked them up all round

her bed. She is hemmed in by them! She has brought *104* videos with her. More than enough for eight weeks, but she says it is best to be on the safe side. What she means by this, I have no idea. I'm sure Mum won't be away longer than eight weeks; she was dithering even as we packed her into the car. But there is absolutely *no need*, we are perfectly capable of looking after ourselves. We have tins in the cupboard and food in the fridge, and Auntie Jay has said that every weekend we are to go downstairs and eat with her. Whatever happens, we will not starve!

This evening was a real dinner party. Very grown up! Auntie Jay said, "I'm giving it in your honour, I've invited everyone in the house." We weren't quite sure who else was in the house, but thought we had better get dressed up, just in case.

"It's probably only old people," said Tash.

"Yeah," I said, "like married couples."

"On the other hand, you never can tell."

She didn't have to explain what *that* meant! It meant, you never can tell when there might be a boy… Me and Tash practically live inside each other's heads, we can always tune in to what the other is thinking – though perhaps upon reflection that's not so difficult, since it usually concerns boys! We are on the lookout for boys wherever we go. On the way in to school, on the way back from school, in the shopping centre, even on the

building site in Gliddon Road, where we once saw Justin Timberlake pushing a wheelbarrow. Big day! It wasn't really Justin Timberlake, of course, but it sure did look like him. You just never know when someone gorgeous is going to pop up, and that being the case it seems only sensible to be prepared. Tash and I wouldn't be seen dead wearing last year's washed-out fashion statements! We dressed with as much care for Auntie Jay's dinner party as we would for a rave.

"It's only polite," I said.

"Exactly," said Tash.

And then we both looked at Ali and went, "*Ali!*" We screamed it at her. "*You're not going like that?*"

Ali said, "Like what?"

Well! Like a derelict, if she

really wanted to know. A horrible old saggy T-shirt and striped cotton trousers that *ballooned* round the bum.

"Haven't you got anything better?" I wailed.

Ali seemed bewildered. She said, "It's only Auntie Jay."

And all the other people in the house… who *knew* what kind of gorgeous male might be there? I didn't say this to Ali, however; there wouldn't have been any point. She is so immature! It's like, for her, boys are still an alien species. And to think she is almost fourteen!!!

Anyway, as it happened there wasn't a gorgeous male in sight. Mostly it was what we had predicted: Auntie Jay's friend, Jo Dainty; a married couple that live on the ground floor called Anne and Robert (quite nice but *very boring*), and a man from the second floor, directly beneath us, who is called Andrew and wears cardigans. Well, that's what he was wearing tonight, all shapeless and woolly. I thought to myself that what he needed was a girlfriend to advise him on such matters and make him a bit more trendy. Auntie Jay, perhaps? She is unattached, and she obviously shares my views on cardigans cos at one point I heard her whisper, "Andrew, really! I thought you were going to donate that thing to charity?" He was quite shamefaced and clutched at his grungy old cardy with both hands in a defensive kind of way, as if she might be going to snatch it off him right there and then. I felt quite sorry for him. Auntie Jay can be really bossy!

Now I have come to the part which I have been dying to write. We have a piece of Extremely Interesting Information. In fact it is the BIG NEWS of the day: *the cardigan man has a son who lives with him.*

A boy! A real boy! Under the same roof! He was out with his friends this evening and so didn't come to our little dinner party, boo hoo! And to think we got all dressed up... Of course we have no idea what he is like, he may be a total geek, but you can see that the cardigan man must have been quite fanciable when he was young, so we have high hopes. The annoying thing is that Ali – of all people – has actually met him. What a waste! She came back upstairs literally *five minutes* ahead of us, which means we only just missed him. She wouldn't even have thought to tell us if she hadn't heard me and Tash eagerly speculating what he might be like. All casually she goes, "I just bumped into him on the stairs."

 Breathlessly, Tash said, "What's he like?"

Ali shrugged. "Just a boy."

"How old is he?"

"Dunno," said Ali.

"Didn't ask."

"How old does he *look*?"

"Dunno. 'Bout my age?"

Yessss!!! Needless to say, we pumped like crazy, trying to find out whether he was gorgeous or geeky, but Ali is just *so* unsatisfactory. All she could say was, "He's got brown hair." The only thing she noticed... brown hair!

"Well, that's cool," said Tash.

"Yeah, like really unusual," I said.

We were being sarcastic, but sarcasm rolls right off Ali.

She said, "I only saw him for about two seconds."

Well. Two seconds is all that me and Tash would need!

"Do you think you would recognise him if you saw him again?" I said. Still being sarcastic.

"I'm not sure," said Ali. "I might do." She was being *serious*!

Tomorrow is Sunday, so with any luck we shall manage to catch a glimpse for ourselves. We plan on going up and down the stairs quite a lot, and generally hanging about on the landing.

On the whole, it has been a good day. *Promising*, I think I would call it. It's now eleven o'clock and I am going to lie down. Ali is tucked away in her broom cupboard, with her *Star Treks* and Fat Man, and I am here in the big bed with Tash. Tash is giggling and twitching her toes. She had better not twitch in the night!

Sunday

She did! She twitched! In the middle of the night I woke up to find the bottom of the duvet dancing a jig. I had to kick her before she would stop. When I taxed her with it, she said that I'd made whiffling noises with my mouth.

"Like this!" And she began blowing air bubbles through her lips, like a goldfish.

I don't believe that I whiffled. She is just saying it to get back at me! She definitely twitched because why else would the duvet have been going up and down? We are not going to fall out over it, however; me and Tash never fall out. In any case, as Tash so wisely said, it's good practice for when we get married.

Talking of marriage… we still haven't seen The Boy. I went up and down the stairs seventeen times, and hung about like mad on the landing, but he never appeared. But we have discovered his name! It is Gus. Gus O'Shaugnessy. We got O'Shaugnessy off the downstairs doorbell, otherwise I most probably wouldn't have known how to spell it. Auntie Jay told us that he was called Gus. A good name! We think it's really neat. Far more promising than, say, Kevin or Shane. I'm thinking of Kevin Trodd who lives in our road and is the sort of

boy that would cut worms in half, just to see if they wriggled, and Shane Mackie who is Avril Mackie's brother and a bit of a nerd. Gus sounds like… well! We shall see. He has to emerge at some stage. When he does, we shall be watching!

We went down to Auntie Jay's again for dinner. Her friend Jo was still there. She is quite funny and sharp and ever so left-wing. Dad would most probably have had a seizure! But me and Tash like her as she makes us laugh, and also she is not at all patronising. Like Anne and Robert last night kept asking us these really dumb questions about which year we were in, and when did we get to take our GCSEs, and what subjects we were best at, and what did we want to do when we left school, yawn yawn. I know they were only trying to be polite but you could tell they really weren't in the least bit interested. Jo doesn't bother with questions, she engages you in conversation and actually listens to what you say. We like that!

Me and Tash, of course, were desperate to learn more about The Boy (which is how we referred to him before we found out his name). However, we didn't want to ask Auntie Jay ourselves in case she got it into her head that we were interested and flew into a Mum-like panic, so we got Ali to do it for us. We gave her strict instructions.

"Don't just go jumping in. Be *discreet*."

"Like how?" said Ali.

"Like sort of… building up slowly," said Tash. "You could ask about his dad, and what he does, and how long he's lived here, and then you could just, like… slip it in."

"*I happened to bump into his son on the stairs last night.* That sort of thing."

"Then what?" said Ali.

"Oh, well, then you could sort of very casually ask what his name was, and how old he is, and where he goes to school, and—" Tash waved a hand. "Stuff like that."

We should have known better than to trust Ali. She has no idea how to be discreet! First off we had to kick her, quite hard, under the table before we could get her going; and then when she did get going she went at it like a mad creature. There wasn't any stopping her!

"What does that man do that lives here? The one that lives underneath us? The one with the son? Has he lived here long?"

"Andrew?" said Auntie Jay. "He moved in last year,

33

after he broke up with his wife. He's a writer, he writes educational books. A very interesting man! He—"

"What about his son?" said Ali.

Oh, God! I nearly died. I saw that Tash had gone bright red.

"What about him?" said Auntie Jay.

"Well, like, what is he called and how old is he, and all that sort of thing."

"*Ali!*" Tash was mouthing at her across the table. I was kicking at her.

"He's fourteen," said Auntie Jay. "His name is Gus. What else would you like to know?"

Ali shot an inquiring glance at Tash. Tash, deliberately, kept her eyes on her plate.

Auntie Jay seemed amused. She said, "How about where he goes to school? Whether he's got a girlfriend?"

"Yes!" Ali beamed, triumphantly, at me. I squirmed. Tash concentrated very hard on shovelling food into her mouth.

"He goes to Simon Standish," said Auntie Jay. "As to whether he's got a girlfriend – " She was laughing at us! " – I'm afraid I really couldn't say. But I'm sure you'll make it your priority to find out!"

At least she didn't fly into a panic and remind us of the No Boys rule. Just to reassure her, however, we have stuck a big sign on the outside of our door:

Ali wanted to know what it meant. She said, "What peril? What would happen if they came in?"

"We'd jump on them!" yelled Tash.

Ali plainly thinks we are mad. But we think she is a total whacko, so that's OK!

Monday

Everyone at school is just *so* envious of us! Meg Hennessy couldn't believe that we are truly independent.

"All on your own?" she kept saying. "Completely on your own?"

Daisy Markham was the only one that wasn't envious. She said she thought that she would be a bit scared if she were left on her own, but as Meg pointed out, "There are three of them. It must be such fun!"

Daisy still seemed doubtful. She really is a complete wimp. She said, "I can't imagine my parents leaving me to look after myself."

Like this was some kind of criticism of Mum and Dad. I resented that! I said, "Mum knows she can trust us."

"Yes, and it's good training," said Tash.

"But you could get up to *anything*," said Daisy.

"Like we might have orgies," I said; and me and Tash went off into a fit of the screaming giggles.

Tuesday

Kim Rogers asked us today if we were going to take the opportunity to have a party. Tash said, "You bet!" It is in fact no.1 on our list of things to do. We'll have to check it out with Auntie Jay, of course, but I'm sure she'll say that we can. She might even let us invite boys, if it's a party! After all, you can't really have one without them. I have to say that Auntie Jay is pretty relaxed about most things. She has made up one or two rules that we have to follow, but they are mostly just common sense, such as always being sure to tell her if we are going out and where we are going. She has put a book on the hall table – the In-and-Out Book. We sign out, and sign in! We're cool with this. Just because we are teenagers – almost – does not make us unreasonable. It's only when grown-ups are unreasonable that we take umbrage. That is *such* a good word! Umbrage, umbrage. I have just said it to Tash, who says that she has never heard of it.

"What's it mean?"

I said, "It means when you get the hump."

Tash said that she had the hump right now, with Ali. "She's doing baked beans again. She did baked beans last night. We'll get bean-bound!"

We are taking it in turns to do the cooking, and this week it's Ali's turn. I'm all for cutting down on the workload, but I do think that baked beans two nights in a row is a bit much. I have just said this to Ali. I said, "Can't you do something different?"

"Like what?" said Ali.

I said, "I dunno! Omelettes, or fish fingers, or something."

Ali said that that would mean cooking. She said, "I told you before, I don't cook. I just open tins."

I said, "Well, couldn't you at least have opened some other kind of tin?"

Honestly! It's like she never even thought of it. Primly, she said that now she had opened the beans, we would have to eat them.

"You can't waste food."

I suggested she fed them to Fat Cat, but they are in tomato sauce and tomato sauce, it seems, is bad for cats.

"This is going to look really great in my Food Diary," said Tash. "Monday: beans. Tuesday: beans. Wednesday—"

"Beans are good for you," said Ali.

 Tash said, "Beans give you wind." And she pursed her lips and made a long, loud growly noise. I immediately did the same.

"That is so rude," said Ali.

Tash said, "Beanz meanz fartz!" and we both collapsed.

Wednesday

Email from Mum. She says she is not going to email us every day, just once a week, and she would like us to email her back once a week. We have delegated this task to Ali. We feel it is the least she can do (to make up for the beans) and have told her that it will be good for her. She was quite meek about it and promised that tonight she will open a different kind of tin.

Me and Tash have just been down to see Auntie Jay and ask her about the party. She has said yes. Hooray! She has also said that we can invite whoever we want, *including boys*, but that a) it will have to finish by nine o'clock and b) she will have to look in on us every now and again, just to check.

"I won't cramp your style, don't worry! But I did promise your mum I'd keep an eye on you."

The party is to be on Saturday week. We are quite excited! We have already made out a list of the people

we intend to invite. They are: Meg Hennessy, Kim Rogers, Zoella Barling, Ishara Khan, Avril Mackie and Shauna Bates. Meg, Kim and Zoella because we are particular friends with them, the other three because they have brothers! Ishara's is rather plain and has spots, and Avril's is a bit of a nerd, but Shauna's is quite nice, and in any case we reckon that any boys are better than no boys at all. We are not inviting Daisy Markham because we don't think she deserves it, and anyway she doesn't have any brothers.

"What about him downstairs?" said Tash.

A knotty problem! We still haven't set eyes on him. It's really annoying as we are for ever racing up and down the stairs or out on to the landing. We have found a secret way of referring to him, for when Ali is around. We refer to him as "Gosh". From his name: **G**us **O'SH**aughnessy. Pretty neat, we think! The way it works is like this. One of us, Tash for instance, will come into the room, and I will go, "Gosh?" meaning, "Did you see him?" and she will shake her head, meaning "No I didn't." Then a few minutes later it will be my turn. I will stand up, and stretch, and say, "*Gosh*," meaning, "Now I am going to go and have a look." And Ali will be completely mystified! I suppose it is a bit mean, keeping her in the dark, but really she is not in the least bit interested. Tash and I are just waiting for the day when one of us bursts in and cries, "Gosh!!!" meaning that at long last there has been a sighting.

We could, of course, just go downstairs and knock on the door and give him an invitation. We have discussed this, but Tash is worried in case he turns out to be hideous. I said, "How hideous could he be?" and we speculated for a while, and frightened ourselves with visions of a Kevin Trodd type creature, so now we have decided that we will give him until the weekend to show himself. If by then we still haven't managed to check him out we shall have to ask Auntie Jay. We would really rather not as we know she'll only laugh, but we certainly don't want any Kevin Trodds turning up!

Thursday

Meg has promised that she will try to get her cousin Tom to come to the party and Zoella says that she knows a boy she can bring, so things are definitely starting to look up! We asked Ali this evening who she's going to invite. She said she hadn't thought of inviting anyone. She thought it was our party, not hers.

It made us feel guilty, when she said that. We do have this tendency to leave her out of things.

"You must *at least* ask Louise," I said.

Tash said yes, and anyone else she could think of. "Like any boys you might know, for example."

We live in hope!

I have just been reading through Mum's list of Dos and Don'ts, which she stuck on the back of the door before she left. This is the first time I've really looked at them. These are some of the things that we must DO:

. Check cooker is turned off before leaving home

. Check taps are turned off in sink and bath

. Check TV is turned off

. Check windows are closed

. Check door of food cupboard is closed

. Check door of fridge is shut properly.

Oh, and CHECK IN WITH AUNTIE JAY BEFORE GOING TO SCHOOL AND AGAIN ON RETURN. We have had long lectures on that one.

As for the others… all I can say is, well! I can understand about the food cupboard, cos if Fat Man got in there and found anything even remotely consumable he would eat himself silly, but *the door of the fridge*? Pur-lease! Does she really think we are dumb enough to leave a fridge door open???

Still haven't seen him downstairs.

Friday

Got back from school to find huge puddle of water on carpet. Thought at first that Fat Man had had an accident, but not even Fat Man could wee that much. In any case, he has his litter tray in the bathroom. It was Tash  who traced it to the fridge… the door was open just the *tiniest crack*, and all the insides had melted. I cried, "Which blithering idiot didn't shut the door properly?" I knew it couldn't be me. I mean, I had read Mum's list of Do's and Don'ts.

"Who was the last one to go there?" said Tash.

We both looked at Ali.

"Who put the milk away after breakfast?"

"You did," said Ali.

"*Me*?" I was outraged. How dare she blame me? "What about the butter? Who put the butter away?"

"The same person that put the milk away?" said Tash.

It's not true! I'm sure I didn't put the butter away. I didn't even touch the blasted butter. I bet it was Tash!

We have come to the conclusion that there is obviously something wrong with the fridge door, since it takes such a superhuman effort to close it. We'd rather not tell Auntie Jay in case she thinks it's something we've done, so Ali has come up with the bright idea – she gets them, occasionally – of leaving a bucket of water jammed in front of it. It is simple, but it does seem to work. In the meantime we have mopped up the floor and just hope that nothing has leaked down through the ceiling into the O'Shaugnessys' flat, but we don't think it can have done as Mr O'Shaugnessy would surely have been up here complaining?

Still no sighting of Gosh. Is he some kind of recluse???

Week 2, Saturday

Well, it has finally happened. We have seen him! Tash came bursting into the room going, "GOSH!" in tones of great excitement. It was the moment we have been waiting for, and I am pleased to record that I was ready for it. Tash plunged back out, and I immediately plunged after her. We bundled together, bumping and jostling, down the stairs, and there he was, standing in the hall, sorting through the post on the hall table. I think he was quite surprised when we came cantering up. He spun round, dropping a handful of letters as he did so, and it is definitely a case of oo-er, mushy peas and soft ice cream! How Ali could have described him as "just a boy" is quite beyond us. Surely even she could see that he is totally gorgeous? His hair, for instance, is not just a boring brown, as reported by Ali, it is *golden* brown, like he's had highlights put in it, except you can see that it's quite natural. And he has this little dimple thing in his chin, which is just so cute! I am not good at descriptions, but I think it's enough to say that both me and Tash have gone into total meltdown. We have turned to liquid!

Before we liquidised, we managed – just about – to get through our double act. Tash said, "Hi!", beaming fit to bust.

Gus said, "Hi," still seeming a bit, like, startled. I guess we did rush him, rather.

Tash was the one who got in first, though it doesn't actually matter which of us starts cos we know the script off by heart.

"This is my sister, Emily – "

"And this is my sister, Tash."

"You probably don't think we look much like each other?"

"Even though we were born on *exactly the same day*."

"Exactly the same year!"

"Which ought to make us twins."

Pause.

"But we're not!"

Surprise, surprise!

"See, her mum – "

"Married her dad."

"So in point of fact – "

"We are not actually related at all!"

Ho ho! Sometimes people laugh, and sometimes they look kind of nervous, like they think we're a bit mad, or something. Gus just blinked and said, "Cool!"

I nodded. "We think so." And then I nudged at Tash, and she nudged at me, and both together we said, "Would you like to come to a party we're having?"

It's funny how often we find ourselves doing this sort of thing... talking like we're a chorus. We don't do it on purpose; it just seems to happen.

"So would you like to?" said Tash.

Gus said yeah, great, that'd be cool. He then added that in fact he had already been asked. "Just now, by your sister."

"*Ali*?" She'd gone off a few minutes earlier to meet her friend Louise in town. How sneaky of her!

"I suppose she's your sister?" said Gus.

"Yeah," I said, "she's mine." I said it with some reluctance. I am not always that keen on laying claim to Ali. I was desperately trying to remember what she had been wearing and thinking please, *please* not let it be her horrible saggy T-shirt and the bum-baggy trousers again. It creates such a bad impression, when me and Tash try *so* hard to make the best of ourselves.

47

The really important thing, however, is that Gus is coming. Hip, hip, hooray! A boy *all of our own*. Not a cousin or a brother, but a real genuine *boy* invited by us. Well, by Ali, I suppose, but it comes to the same thing.

"Of course, you're the one he'll fancy," moaned Tash, as we came back upstairs and hurled ourselves on to the bed. I don't know why she said that. She is far prettier than I am! I said this to her, and she said that she wasn't, and that in any case I was taller and skinnier and *blonde*.

I said, "But I haven't any boobs," and Tash said that neither had she, and we both heaved big sighs. We think we may have to start doing special exercises. I have read that there are some, and really, if this carries on, I mean this continuing horrible flatness, we shall have to take some kind of drastic action. It is so unfair! Ali has boobs, and doesn't even want them. They're not very big, but at least they are there. And then she goes round all hump-shouldered, as if she's ashamed of them! When I have boobs, even just the tiniest, faintest beginnings of them, I shall make sure that they are – ahem! – well to the fore. So to speak. I shan't show off about them, cos that would be vulgar, but I shall certainly not try to hide them!

Ali has just come in, and oh, God, she *is* wearing the

t-shirt and the baggies! Tash is asking her about Gus. I shall have to stop and listen to this.

OK, we have the story. Ali was on her way out to meet Louise and lo and behold, what happens? She bumps into Gus – *again* – on the stairs.

"You said you wanted boys to come to the party, so I asked him. He didn't seem all that keen so I told him he could bring his girlfriend, if he wanted."

"*What?*" We screeched it at her.

"We don't want *girlfriends*," said Tash.

"Well, it's OK," said Ali, "Cos he hasn't got one. He's coming by himself."

Phew! Relief! That was a nasty moment. I suppose in a way, it has to be said, Ali has done us a favour. Now at least we know there is no competition! Not at his school, either, cos Simon Standish is all-boys. Things are looking good.

Sunday

We have done our first weekly shop! We felt very important, going to Tesco's all by ourselves. We are taking the bus there, but coming back by cab. Mum said this is what we are to do, to save bothering Auntie Jay. Before we went, we made a long list of stuff we had to buy, including boring things such as washing-up liquid and toilet rolls. We were quite proud of ourselves.

Ali said, "Mum *always* buys toilet rolls."

But it is really difficult, thinking what to eat all week – especially as it's my turn to cook! I am already beginning to have a bit more sympathy with Ali and her baked beans, but I am determined to do proper meals and not rely on tins. Mum left us a cook book called "Simple Meals for Busy People" and I have been poring over it. So far I have thought of: pancakes, omelettes, spaghetti, cheese on toast and burgers. I asked Tash if she reckoned these would be OK, but she just waved a hand and said, "Whatever!" She has been preoccupied all day. She says that we are doomed. Last night on the television they had a programme about terrorist attacks and how we all had to be prepared. Tash has really taken it to heart. She told us, as we went into Tesco's, that we must stock up with loads of tins and bottled water.

"And batteries! We have to have batteries!"

Ali (who was off somewhere with Louise and didn't watch the programme) said, "What do we need batteries for?"

Tash cried, "For the radio! And the torch!"

I pointed out that we didn't have a torch. A big mistake, as she immediately insisted on buying one. "A proper one! Not some piddling little thing. If the electricity goes off it's the only light we'll have!"

To set her mind at rest we put a large (and hugely expensive) torch in the trolley, plus some large and hugely expensive batteries to go with it, and this calmed

her down a bit until Ali had to go and point out that we couldn't get batteries for the radio as we didn't know what sort of batteries it used, whereupon Tash cried out hysterically, *in the middle of Tesco's*, that in that case we would have to buy "Lots of batteries, loads of batteries!" A whole selection of batteries.

I said, "But there are dozens."

"Then we'll have to get dozens! You heard what they said… we can't risk being without a radio!"

I had no idea she had taken it so seriously. Well, I mean, it is serious, of course, and I am sure that Mum and Dad would want us to be prepared, but we do have a budget to stick to and I don't think even Mum and Dad would expect us to spend all our money on dozens of useless batteries. In the end we managed to talk her out of it, but only by promising that as soon as we got home we would check the radio and then, on the way back from school tomorrow, we could call in at one of the shops on the High Street.

"After all," I said, "they're not going to come today."

The terrorists, I meant. I was trying to calm her down, but in fact I only succeeded in getting her all agitated again as she has now taken it into her head that they could attack at any moment.

This, unfortunately, happens to be true, and therefore just made *me* agitated, as well. I sometimes think that Ali has the right idea. It must be so much easier to go round with your head in the clouds, blissfully unaware of all the terrible things taking place on this planet.

I am quite surprised at Tash, however; she is obviously a lot more sensitive than I thought. She says that I, on the other hand, am totally *in*sensitive. I wonder if that's right? I don't believe it is as I cried buckets when poor Fat Man got knocked down by a car that time, and we had to rush him to the vet. It's just that you can't let these things take over your life. You would never leave home, or go anywhere, or do anything, but would spend your whole time hiding in a cupboard with bottles of water and batteries.

I said this to Tash and she told me that I have no imagination, which is *certainly* not right. I have a great deal of imagination! So much that I really don't want to think about it, and if you ask me Tash would be better off not thinking about it, too, since it gives her so much grief. I really wish we had never watched the stupid programme in the first place! I would have turned it off if I had known it was going to upset her.

Anyway, what with Tash being so fussed about terrorists, it made her completely useless when it came to planning the week's menu, and Ali wasn't much better. All *she* could think about was getting in enough food for Fat Man. She went off by herself with a basket and came back beaming, with about ninety-eight tins of cat food. She said, "You know how fussy he is… we need to make sure he has plenty of choice."

I peered into the basket, and quite frankly I nearly had a seizure.

"Lobster!" I shrieked. "You've got him lobster!"

Ali said yes, it was a special gourmet cat food. She said a woman she had been talking to in the cat food section had recommended it.

"She gets it for her cats as a treat… she's got ten of them. She says they're like her children. Look! See?

There she is." And she pointed down the aisle at this totally dotty-looking woman pushing a trolley that was full to the brim with cat food.

Why is it that Ali is for ever talking to mad people? Why can't she ever talk to anyone normal? They are always raving nutters, which I know is not politically correct but even Mum says that Ali has a knack. For picking out weirdoes, that is. I mean, honestly! Buying lobster for a cat. I sometimes seriously think that Ali should be kept tethered to either me or Tash, so that every time she starts up one of her zany conversations with someone she can be immediately dragged away. It is such a bad habit! Look where it's got us... a cupboard full of cat tins and practically nothing else.

Tash has just philosophically announced that if the worst comes to the worst we can always eat Whiskas. She is obviously feeling more settled.

Monday

Went downstairs this evening to ask Auntie Jay if she had some bread we could borrow. With all the frenzied buying of bottled water and cat food we clean forgot about it. Bread! The staple of life!!! Auntie Jay wasn't back from work but her friend Jo was there. She said, "You really just want to *borrow* it? What kind of state would it be in when you gave it back?" So then of course I had to explain that I needed it for cheese on toast (my menu for today) and she said in that case she would *give* me a loaf.

"But once you've used it, please don't even think of giving it back… not in any shape or form!"

Jo is really funny. She makes me laugh! I was quite surprised that she was here on a Monday, but according to Ali she has now moved in on a permanent basis.

"The lease ran out on her flat and she needed somewhere in a hurry."

I said, "How do you know?"

Ali said, "Auntie Jay told me."

When did Ali get to speak to Auntie Jay? She is so sneaky! I don't know half the things she gets up to.

The cheese on toast was really tasty. Though I say it myself, and I suppose it may sound a bit like boasting, I believe I may be rather a good cook! For afters we had fresh fruit, which at first made Tash turn her nose up. She said it was "*Boring.*" But I reminded her that we are supposed to eat "a rainbow a day," and I told her to make sure she recorded it in her Food Diary.

"And put whose week it is for cooking!"

Tash promised that she would. She's feeling happier now as we've bought spare batteries for the radio.

Wednesday

Last night in bed me and Tash had a long and intense discussion about Auntie Jay. We think that she and her friend Jo might be *a couple*. In fact we think that they almost certainly are. After all, they are both in their thirties and neither of them are married. And Jo is quite a manly sort of woman. I don't mean that in a derogatory way! I really like her, and we are the hugest fans of Auntie Jay. She is so bright and sassy, and a truly inspiring person to have as your aunt. We don't in the least mind if she is gay! We are not fussed about it. We are very relaxed about anything to do with s.e.x. There is this teacher at school, Ms Meadows, that we are as sure as can be has had a sex change operation. But that's all right! We are quite cool about it. We think it's  interesting and should like to know more.

We are not saying anything about Auntie Jay to Ali as Ali is still so naïve, in spite of being almost fourteen. We wouldn't want to shock her.

This evening, Fat Man ate his lobster. We had spaghetti. Ho hum! I say no more.

Thursday

Bumped into Gosh – Gus! – on our way back from school. Me and Tash, that is. We walked up the road with him and Tash prattled – it's the only word for it! She *prattled* – about the party. Sometimes at school she gets told off for talking too much, and really I am not surprised. She's like a mouth on a stick! Poor Gus couldn't get a word in edgeways, and neither could I. I do hope she hasn't scared him off. There are some boys where it wouldn't matter, as they are convinced they are God's gift and that all girls fancy them like crazy, but Gus is not like that. He's really quiet, so that you do have to make a bit of an effort. You do have to be just a *little* bit forward. That, however, is not to say that you should go way over the top, which is what Tash was doing.

I have said this to her. In spite of being such hugely best friends, we never hesitate to criticise. We take it all in good part! I was not in the least put out the other day, for instance, when Tash told me that "You have a most peculiar walk!" She said she had never noticed it before, but "You lean *backwards*." And she showed me what I looked like, and it made me feel so self-conscious! She said, "I hope you didn't mind, but I thought you ought to know." And I thanked her for drawing it to my attention, and said that I felt grateful to her, because this is what friends ought to do.

I am now trying very hard *not* to lean backwards, and Tash says it's already much better. She has told me that if ever she starts to walk funny, "Or like if my breath smells, or something," I am to be sure to tell her immediately. So I told her about being too forward and she said rather sniffily that that was "a matter of opinion." She said that some boys like girls to take the initiative. I said, "Oh! Is that what you were doing?" Personally I would have said that she was monopolising, but there are those of us that can take criticism and those that can't. I'm afraid Tash is obviously one of the latter. What a disappointment! Just as she was starting to get the tiniest bit on my nerves, however, she fortunately backed down and admitted that I could be right. She then became all humble and wailed that she didn't have any feminine charms and no boy would ever look twice at her.

"Especially not Gosh! I mean, Gus. I'm too up front, aren't I? I'm too pushy. Oh, God! He's bound to prefer you to me!"

I am so relieved that Tash climbed down off her high horse. I was only trying to be helpful! As to which one of us Gus will prefer... well! We shall have to wait and see.

Cooked pancakes tonight, but something went wrong. They turned all grey and leathery, and squeaked when I prodded them. How can a pancake squeak???

Tash and Ali said they couldn't eat them, so I was forced to open a tin of ravioli. At least it wasn't beans!

Friday

Everyone at school is hugely excited about the party. We are, too. I suspect it will be a little different from the one we had last year, with Mum and Dad benignly hovering, and not a boy in sight! Of course, we were only just twelve. We have matured a lot since then.

Spent all evening deciding what to wear. Tash thinks her red ra-ra skirt with a halter top and her trainers. I think so, too. Short skirts really suit her!

I am probably going for my floaty gypsy skirt with my new wrap top. Either that or my denim fishtail. I can't make up my mind!

If I wear the denim it means I could wear my canvas boots to go with it. I just love those boots! On the other hand, the gypsy skirt is more flattering. Also more romantic!

I am going to sleep on it.

Week 3, Saturday
Auntie Jay is so lovely! She has provided all the food and drink for our party.

She said, "I wasn't sure what you'd want, so I just bought a bit of everything. It should be enough, do you think?"

We were completely knocked out! I said that it would be enough to feed an entire army, and Auntie Jay laughed and said that if teenagers of today were anything like when she was young, they would "go at it like a horde of locusts". We have spread it all out on the table and can't stop gloating over it. Tash said it made her feel safe to have it there. She said she had woken up in the middle of the night and started worrying about terrorists again. What worries her now is in case they come on a Friday or Saturday, before we've done the shopping. Very earnestly she told me that "The best day would be a Sunday, cos then we'd have stocked up."

Honestly! I really thought she had got over this obsession. I know it's frightening, but there is no point in dwelling on it. We have to get on with our lives. That is what they did in New York; they didn't let themselves be defeated. I said this to Tash. I said, "I think it's important that we show our utter contempt and carry on the same as normal, otherwise it will mean that they've won."

I expected her to argue, or tell me once again that I was insensitive, but to my surprise she said that I was quite right. She said, "From now on, I am simply going to forget about it." I told her that that was the best idea she had had in a long time, and suggested that we turn our thoughts to something more frivolous, such as the party. Tash said, "Parties aren't frivolous... we might meet Gorgeous Boys." And then she clapped a hand to her mouth and said, "You know what? We haven't check what Ali's going to wear!"

Omigod! So we hadn't. Left to herself, Ali is likely to be a complete disaster. We immediately prised her away from the computer and demanded that we go through her wardrobe. She spends way too much time on that computer, if you ask me. Getting broadband was a BIG MISTAKE. Surfing the net is not real life! I do sometimes worry about Ali. How can she ever hope to find a boyfriend if she isn't interested in clothes, or make-up, or how she looks? If she does nothing but watch her *Star Trek* videos and mess around in cyberspace? She needs to get out there and get a life!

Tash said, "Ali, it's for your own good."

Well, it is! I know we're partly thinking of ourselves, cos it is so utterly cringe-making when she turns up looking like she's just crawled out of a compost heap; but mainly we are thinking of what is best for her. Surely even Ali must feel better when she's dressed nicely?

She does *have* decent stuff in her wardrobe; Mum makes sure of that. She just never wears it! It's not what you would call ultra chic, cos Mum has no idea and neither does Ali, but at least it's not cringe-making. The only problem is, she hasn't brought very much with her. She said, "I didn't think I'd need it." Like we were going into hibernation for two months? Of course, if Ali had her way she probably would go into hibernation.

We took out everything there was and laid it on the bed. Then we looked at each other.

"Well! She can't wear any of *this*," said Tash. "Except, maybe… " She pulled out a pair of cord trousers. "These aren't so bad. The colour's a bit naff—"

Pink. That was Mum. She has this fixed idea that all young people should to go round looking like maypoles. She just hates it when me and Tash wear black!

Tash said, "What d'you reckon?"

I said the trousers would just about pass, but as for any of the tops – forget it! Saggy vests, droopy T-shirts… In the end, I very nobly sacrificed my wrap top.

It's the only thing I have that even remotely fits her. Even so, it's a tidge on the small side, but not so's you'd notice. I think she looks really good in it. Really sophisticated. I said this to her, and in doubtful tones she said, "You're not just saying it?"

I said, "No! I mean it."

Ali said, "You don't think it's too tight?"

"It's not too tight," said Tash. "It's a perfect fit! It shows off your boobs."

Well! That was *absolutely* the wrong thing to say. It took me a good ten minutes to calm her down and convince her that she looked ace. Which she does! Ali can be really pretty if she just takes a bit of trouble with herself. Tash wanted to style her hair, so we looked through *Glam Girl* until we found something we  thought would suit her. It's really cool! We've taken two long bits from the side and sort of twisted them into ropes and tied them in a knot on top of her head. It looks *so* much better than having it all hanging about like she usually does.

Ali, needless to say, is in a dither and says it feels "peculiar", but we have given her strict instructions *not to fiddle with it*. I told her to go and watch a *Star Trek* while we got dressed, so that is what she's doing, shut away in her broom cupboard with Fat Man. I'm hoping that *Star Trek* will take her mind off her hair.

Me and Tash, meanwhile, have prinked and preened and paraded in front of each other and are now ready and waiting. We have sorted out a load of CDs and we have a lava lamp which Auntie Jay has lent us. She said she'd rather we didn't use candles as she's scared of the house being set alight. In any case, it won't really get dark enough, even with the curtains closed. I wish we could have started later and gone on till midnight, but I know that is too much to hope for. Mum would certainly not let us.

Tash has just been so sweet! She said to me that I looked "mouth-wateringly" gorgeous. That was *such* a nice thing to say. I told her in return that she looked like a ravishing rock chick (a phrase I read in *Glam Girl*). I could see that she was pleased by this.

"But he'll still prefer you to me," she moaned.

Why does she think so??? I do believe I look a bit more romantic (floaty skirt) but Tash *definitely* looks more sexy. I told her this, and her face lit up. She said, "Do I? Do I really?"

I said, "Yes, short skirts are always sexy."

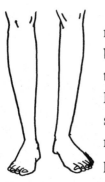

The only reason I'm not wearing one is because of my horrible thighs. They are all thin, like drainpipes. No shape at all! Tash's are nice and round and plump, and if she whirls about really fast you get a glimpse of her knickers. (Calvin Klein, natch!) Dad would be horrified. But he's not here, and Auntie Jay has been up to inspect us and has said that we both look "very pretty".

Now it's nearly time. I have butterflies in my stomach! Which of us will he go for???

Full report tomorrow…

Sunday

He didn't go for either of us. Not me *or* Tash. And Ali disgraced us utterly. She brought shame on us! We just wanted to die. Apart from that, it was a great party; everybody said so. Even Shauna Bates, who considers herself "a cut above" just because her dad is a TV producer. She told us it was one of the best parties she'd been to in a long time. It was just me and Tash that couldn't enjoy it properly. And it was all Ali's fault!

We are *so* cross with her. We are absolutely furious with her. After all the trouble we went to! She was still in her broom cupboard when Gus arrived (the first one to do so). We didn't mind that as it meant we could have him to ourselves for a bit. We were getting on quite well, telling him all about Mum and Dad, and school, and how we were doing all our own shopping and cooking. He was really impressed, you could tell. Then the door of the broom cupboard opened, and Ali came out, and we nearly sank through the floor. She was wearing her baggy trousers with a horrible old dishrag of a T-shirt! As if that wasn't bad enough she'd gone and undone the whole of our beautiful hair arrangement, so that all these limp strands were now hanging like a pair of shredded curtains round her face. What did she look like??? A total MESS.

Gus said, "Oh. Hi." Me and Tash just stared. We couldn't believe it! All our hard work for nothing.

Ali said she didn't realise that Gus had arrived. She said, "I've been watching *Star Trek*."

Like anybody cared! Gus, being polite, said, "*Next Generation*?"

It doesn't do to encourage Ali. Before we knew it she was off and running. "*DS9*. It's really exciting, they've just mined the wormhole! Captain Sis—"

We had to put a stop to it, she'd have bored him to death.

"Ali," I said. I clawed up a load of papers that she'd left piled all over the computer table and shoved them at her. "I thought you were going to clear this junk away?"

Ali said, "Oh. Yes. Sorry," and promptly scattered the whole lot on the floor. We all got down on our hands and knees to pick them up. I was *seething* with fury, and

I could tell that Tash was, too. I was specially seething because I had sacrificed my wrap top, all to no purpose! (I wore my green embroidered waistcoat, instead. It actually goes quite well with the floaty skirt.)

As we stood up, Gus said, "Is this a red dwarf?"

I couldn't think what he was talking about. He was holding out a sheet of paper, with some messy kind of picture on it. Tash snatched it from him and thrust it at Ali.

"It's some of her astrology stuff. She gets it off the computer. *Are you going to go and put it away?*"

Quite honestly, we just wanted to be rid of her. I'd have been happy if she'd spent the whole evening in her broom cupboard. She wasn't fit to be let out! Specially not when me and Tash were trying so hard to create a good image. I mean, you have to work at these things. It's no use expecting boys to take notice of you if you're not prepared to make some kind of effort.

Ali took the papers, but she didn't go and put them away. She said, "It's astronomy, not astrology."

"Whatever," said Tash.

"Astronomy is stars," said Ali. "Astrology is rubbish."

I beg to differ! I always read my horoscope, and quite often what it says has come true. I'm sure there is something in it. But Ali can be so obstinate at times! She must have known she was putting us to shame, but nothing would budge her. She just went on standing there, clutching her papers to her chest and mouthing on about red dwarves, as if anyone was in the least bit interested. Poor Gus must have wondered what he had got himself into. I mean, this was supposed to be a party, for heaven's sake! You don't expect some lunatic in baggy trousers and a shapeless T-shirt to start lecturing you.

It was a good party, in spite of Ali, but we are still very angry with her. It's simply not worth trying to help some people.

"Why did you do it?" shrieked Tash, when everybody had gone.

Ali said, "I didn't feel comfortable... I didn't feel like me."

Absolutely no remorse! No acknowledgement that she had embarrassed us in front of other people. Fortunately most of our friends know about her, they know that she is what Mum calls "a one-off". She has a sort of reputation at school for being brilliant but weird. I mean, it *is* weird, it is *seriously* weird to appear at a party in grungy old washed-out clothes when you know that everyone else is going to be dressed up. It is weird not to care how you look or what people think of you. We didn't so much mind about Meg, and Zoella, and the others seeing her, but I could just dig a hole and bury myself right now at the thought of Gus knowing she is my sister! It is one of those times when I would like to disown her. I know that I can't, because of promising Mum that we would watch out for her, and I do love her, deep down, but why oh why can't she be more like the rest of us?

Tash and I are still conducting a post mortem. We have discussed at great and satisfying length what everyone was wearing, and how everyone behaved, and who hit it off with who, or whom, or whatever it is, but always, in the end, we come back to Gus. It wasn't like he wasn't friendly, but you can tell when a boy is interested and when he isn't, there are signs that give it away. It's called "body language". I read about it in *Glam Girl*. Like, for instance, if you're talking to a boy at a party and he keeps his eyes fixed on you, that means you can score three points cos he's definitely attracted. If on the other hand his eyes start to wander – forget it!

Gus's eyes didn't exactly wander, but they certainly weren't fixed on me. I just had this feeling that he was being… *polite.* Tash said she had the same feeling when she tried talking to him. She swears she wasn't too forward, and I believe her.

"So what did we do wrong?" she wailed.

I said glumly that we didn't do anything wrong. "He just doesn't fancy us."

"*Neither* of us?"

I said it looked that way. The only consolation is that he didn't seem to fancy anyone else, either, so we reckon we are still in with a chance. At any rate, we do not intend to give up!

Monday

Everyone at school has been talking about the party and saying how good it was. Meg wanted to know where we had found "the yummy boy". She said she could have gone for him big time if he hadn't already been spoken for.

"I mean, like, he belongs to one of you, right?"

Kim immediately pounced and said, "Which one? Who's going out with the yummy boy?"

Me and Tash sort of hummed and hah'd and said that we hadn't yet decided. Kim said, "You haven't, or he

hasn't?" Tash pointed out that we had only met him a few days ago.

"We've hardly had a chance to speak to him properly yet."

Kim did this exaggerated rolling thing with her eyes. She said, "How long do you need?"

Rather sourly, cos I did resent her tone, I said, "I s'ppose you'd have eloped with him by now?"

Kim giggled and said, "Something like that!" It put me in a bad mood for the rest of the day. That girl can be so positively *annoying* at times. Tash agrees with me. We talked about it on the way home.

"Considering she doesn't have a boyfriend at all," said Tash.

"Not unless you count that weedy thing she brought with her."

"That wasn't a boyfriend," said Tash, "that was an *exchange student*."

I said, "Yeah, right. She's got some nerve!"

All the same, we think perhaps she has a point; you can't just sit around waiting for things to happen. There comes a time when you have to take action. We are now going to take it! As from tomorrow we are going to make a *concerted effort*. That is, both of us together. We are not sure yet what we are going to do, but we are certainly going to do something!

Tuesday

Day one of our concerted effort. It has not *quite* gone according to plan, but through absolutely no fault of ours.

Tash said that we had to find some way of drawing attention to ourselves. "But not *obviously*. You know? Like just by chance. Accidentally."

So I put my brain to work and I came up with this cunning notion, a scheme, I suppose you would call it, of how to get ourselves invited in to the O'Shaugnessy abode. It was totally my idea! I was the one that thought of it. Tash merely put the finishing touches. She was the one responsible for the ice cream: *I* had been going to use butter.

I took her through it, step by step. "We get the butter – right? Then we drop it out the window – splat! It lands on the balcony. *Their* balcony. Yeah? So we have to get it back, right? So—"

Tash said, "Hang about, hang about! What are we chucking butter out the window for?"

Patiently – though to be honest I thought she was being a bit slow on the uptake – I explained. "The butter has *fallen* out of the window. Yeah? Accidentally. By mistake. The butter – has fallen—"

"Yeah yeah yeah," said Tash. "I got that bit. What I don't understand is what the butter is *doing* falling out of the window?"

"The butter," I said, "is on the window ledge."

"Doing what?"

I said, "I don't know! Does it matter?"

Tash said yes, it did. She said she had never heard of butter being on a window ledge. "Sounds a bit phoney, if you ask me."

I was getting just a tidge irritated by now, but to keep her happy I went and looked in the freezer, and found a tub of ice cream, and she said that that would do OK. She seemed to think that ice cream on a window ledge was a bit more believable than butter – "We're melting it, yeah? For supper." So I agreed that we could drop ice cream if that was what she preferred, it really didn't matter *what* we dropped so long as we dropped something – and so long as it landed on the balcony. I still say it was basically a good idea. Simple, like all good ideas. Practically fool proof. What could go wrong?

I let Tash do the dropping, being as she is a bit of a sports nut and more likely to hit the target. The tub of ice cream landed with a satisfying *thonk!* right in the middle of the balcony. We waited a couple of minutes, then went tearing downstairs – according to plan – to knock at the door. I should say that I did actually *volunteer* to go by myself, but Tash wouldn't have it.

She said, "No, we're in this together." I guess she was scared of me getting to talk to Gus before she did. I personally thought it looked a bit sinister, the pair of us beaming away on the doorstep, but as it happened it really didn't matter. Nobody was there!

So much for foolproof.

"Now what do we do?" moaned Tash.

I said that we would try again later. "Someone's bound to be there soon!"

But they weren't. Not at five thirty, or six thirty, or seven thirty. Tash said it had been a totally rubbish idea from the start and I'd just better not complain about lack of pudding tomorrow night. She seemed to imply that it was *my* fault the ice cream was lying outside on the balcony, melting.

A few minutes ago (it is now half-past eight) Ali came in. She was carrying the ice-cream tub… *empty*. Tash yelled, "Where did you get that from?"

Ali said, "Gus gave it to me. Is it ours?"

I rushed across to peer out of the window. Sure enough, the tub had gone. In its place was a puddle of strawberry-coloured slush. Tomorrow night's pudding!

"*Did he invite you in?*" said Tash.

Ali seemed surprised. She said no, she had been on her way upstairs when Gus had appeared on the landing, holding the empty tub. "He didn't know whether it was something that belonged to us or whether it had fallen out of an aeroplane." She then said that he had been going to *come up here and ask us*.

In other words, if it hadn't been for Ali arriving at just the wrong moment, my plan would have worked! I knew it was foolproof. Well, almost. We would at least have got to speak to him. We could have invited *him* to come in. Trust Ali!

I have told Tash, however, that all is not lost as we can still go downstairs tomorrow night, as planned.

"We can go and apologise!" I said.

Fretfully, Tash said, "But he won't ask us in."

I said, "He might."

"Why should he?" wailed Tash. "There won't be any reason! Not unless you're planning on dropping more ice cream."

I was about to say that we don't have any more to drop, but decided against it. Tash is being quite negative enough already. Somewhat huffily I said, "Next time *you* can think of something." I don't see why it should always be me.

Wednesday

Day two of concerted effort. Went downstairs to apologise. As planned. By me. *So* frustrating! Door opened by Mr O'Shaugnessy. He is quite a nice man, but obviously has no imagination whatsoever, cos when we started on our double act – which as I have said before is just something that happens, it's not like we do it on purpose – he simply *draped* there, blocking the doorway, ruining any chance we might have had of seeing Gus. Or of him seeing us, for that matter.

Tash explained that we had come to apologise. "For last night."

"For the butter."

"For the *ice* cream."

"The ice cream! On the balcony."

"The balcony!"

"It dropped there – "

"Off the window ledge!"

"It was *so* kind of Gus to give it back."

"We just wanted to say thank you – "

"To say sorry."

"To say thank you *and* sorry. For all the mess – "

"The mess –"

"Such a terrible mess!"

"We do *so* hope it didn't ruin his clothes!"

Well! You would have thought by now he would have been starting to get the message. But no! He just went on standing there. He did open the door a bit wider, but he didn't invite us in. He said, "Ah… the ice cream! We wondered how it had got there."

Earnestly, I explained that we had been melting it. "For supper." Tash, on a note of true inspiration, then suggested that perhaps we could go in and scrub the balcony. I cried, "Yes! Scrub the balcony."

I mean, really, we couldn't have made ourselves

much plainer. But Mr O'Shaugnessy seems a very vague sort of man. He was wearing his woolly cardigan again, and these horrible crumpled old chinos. He needs a woman in his life! I was just about to say that we really did *yearn* to go and scrub his balcony, like we were really *desperate* to scrub his balcony, when suddenly we caught sight of Gus in the background. Immediately we both shrieked, "Hi, Gus!" and danced up and down and waved madly through the gap in the door. Gus turned, and said, "Oh, hi there," and waved back – and promptly disappeared.

His dad said that it was good of us to call, and he was glad that the mystery was solved. He said, "Mind you don't go wasting any more ice cream!" and to my horror I saw the door start to close.

Tash cried, "But the balcony!" It came out in a kind of pathetic bleat.

Gus's dad said not to worry about the balcony; the balcony was fine.

"It rained in the night, if you remember."

He then told us to be sure and come down if there was ever anything we needed, and that was that. End of effort no.2. And we went to so much trouble making ourselves presentable! I even washed my hair. Tash even put on *make-up*, which I personally think is a mistake as she is quite attractive enough without it, but she says she needs it to boost her confidence, so who am I to argue?

We are now feeling THWARTED. But we do not intend to give up! True love, as Tash says, will always find a way. Not that either of us is actually suffering the pangs of love – as *yet*. But speaking for myself I do feel that it may only be a matter of time...

Thursday

Day three of concerted effort. Avril Mackie told us this morning that the week after we come back from half term it's her birthday, and on the Saturday she is going to have a big birthday bash at a pizza restaurant and would we like to come?

"And bring the yummy boy!"

Everyone is now referring to Gus as "the yummy boy". Needless to say, we have assured Avril that we would *love* to go to her party and that *of course* we will bring the yummy boy.

"If we can get him to come," said Tash, as we made our way home after school. "*If* we can ever get to talk to him." I suggested that maybe we should put a note under his door, and so this is what we have done. We typed it on the computer, all sweetly decorated with little pretty party icons, balloons and streamers and those things that you blow and they shoot out. Oh, and we have put RSVP at the bottom and the numbers of *both* our mobiles. As Tash says, "It will be pure chance which of us he rings."

I said, "That's right. If he rings my number it doesn't necessarily mean he prefers me to you." Tash said it hardly could, since he wouldn't know which number was which.

Anyway, we have sneaked downstairs and pushed it under the door and are expecting him to ring at any moment.

I wonder where Ali is? She's always coming and going and doing her own thing. I do wish she would keep us informed!

Friday

We are not going to make any more concerted effort. We have sadly come to the conclusion that we are fighting a losing battle. Gus didn't ring either of our numbers. Instead, he pushed a reply under *our* door. We think he must have done it after we had gone to bed, or early in the morning before we got up, as it was there waiting for us when we woke. It is quite a nice note. It is very friendly and polite. But it's still what Tash calls "a brush off". Well! This is what it says.

Dear Emily and Tash,

Thank you very much for the invitation. I really appreciate you thinking of me but unfortunately I cannot come on that Saturday and so I am afraid that I will have to say no. But thank you again for asking.

Yours sincerely,

Gus O'Shaugnessy.

We must have read it about a million times. At intervals during the day, we have been going up to each other and saying, "Can I have another look?" Like first it would be Tash that was carrying it around, and then it would be me. It is true to say we know it off by heart.

We have had a long discussion about it. Tash pointed out that he didn't have to say "Gus O'Shaugnessy".

"Just Gus would have done."

We wondered if there was any significance attached to this. I suggested he was just trying to be polite, while Tash maintains that it is part of the brush off. I said, "But why should he want to brush us off?" It's not like we are diabolically ugly or have bad breath or anything.

We thought about this for a moment, then very solemnly Tash said, "It's obvious… he's gay."

Of course! As soon as she said it, I knew that she was right. It's the only thing that makes sense.

"I could understand him not going for me," said Tash, "but if he doesn't even go for *you*—"

"If he doesn't even go for *you*," I said. "You are heaps prettier than I am!"

"But you're so lovely and slim!"

"But you have this dear little round face."

"But you're blonde! And I'm so *stunted*."

"Neither of us have boobs," I said. "You don't think that's what's put him off?"

Tash said no, he didn't strike her as being the sort of boy that was fixated on boobs. She said, "You can always tell." I don't know how you can always tell, but

I am prepared to take her word for it. Plus she reminded me that he didn't show any interest in anyone else that came to the party.

"Not even Meg, and she's already a B cup!"

The conclusion seems inescapable; he is simply not interested in girls. We are very cool about it, of course, though it does seem rather a waste – from our point of view. I have to say, however, that we both feel a great deal better now that we have solved the mystery!

Week 4, Saturday
Me and Tash went and mooched round the shops, trying to find something to wear for Avril's birthday bash,

but we were both in the sort of mood where nothing ever looks quite right so that you just can't make up your mind and in the end you don't buy anything at all and go back home feeling like it has all been a total waste of time.

We did get a few bits and pieces, like Tash got a glittery bangle and I got some rainbow nail varnish, but we are still stuck with the same tired old clothes that we have had for ever. We need something new!!! I once read somewhere that if you want to stay fresh and sparkly you have to "re-invent" yourself every now and again, and I am sure this is right. Otherwise, I mean, you just grow stale. I once said this to Mum. I said, "I've worn everything in my wardrobe at least three times!" I meant for birthdays and stuff, not just ordinary every day. I actually went to some trouble to explain to Mum that if I didn't keep "re-inventing", I would end up sitting in the corner like a faded pot plant with people just walking by and chucking all their rubbish on me, not even noticing.

To which Mum said, "Utter nonsense!" She said, "There is such a thing as personality, you know."

There may well be, but personality has to be watered occasionally, just like pot plants. I feel at the moment that I am all dried up. Tash says that she is all dried up, too. We think it's probably the after-effect of receiving *the brush off*. Like some kind of delayed shock. We have never received the brush off before! Tash said, "Of course, it's not his fault. People can't help how they're made."

I said, "No, we could be real groovy chicks and he still wouldn't go for us." We then instantly lapsed into gloom and self-doubt, thinking how we still had nothing decent to wear to Avril's bash.

"And there are bound to be boys there!" wailed Tash.

We've decided that we will go shopping again, maybe at half term, when we are feeling more positive. And this time we'll shop till we drop! Or at any rate until we've found something worth wearing. We are now feeling a bit more cheerful. After all, as Tash says, Gus is not the only pebble on the beach. If only he weren't so utterly gorgeous!

Sunday

I am beginning to understand why it is that Mum always groans when she has to do the shopping. I used to think she was mad. Shopping is fun! But buying toilet rolls and washing-up liquid in Tesco is not exactly what I would call a stimulating experience. The first few times it was, like, really novel, and we had this sort of prideful glow, congratulating ourselves on being so responsible. Mum would be proud of us! Today it was just a drag.

It is Ali's turn on food duty and we watched with mounting gloom as she lobbed tins of baked beans and spaghetti hoops into the trolley. She obviously sensed our growing hostility.

"What?" she said. "What is it?"

"Tinned wind," said Tash, pointing at the beans.

Ali said well, all right, if we didn't like beans, choose something else.

"I want proper food!" roared Tash.

I said yes, me, too. We made a stand, right there in Tesco's.

"Proper food, proper food! We – want – proper – food!"

I suppose it was a bit show-offy of us, but at least we shamed Ali into putting the tins back on the shelf. She said, "OK, I'll do cheese and eggs and stuff, but if you want *real cooking* we'll have to do it together cos I don't cook!"

Like I've said before, she can be really stubborn. A guy that was walking past heard her say about not cooking. He wagged a finger at her, all mock reproving, and said, "That's no way to keep a man happy!" We thought that was extremely sexist. Poor Ali went bright red; it made us feel quite sorry for her. I mean, really, it was just *so* humiliating. And like anyone would want to keep a man  happy that way! Dressing nicely and making the most of yourself is different; that gives you good feelings and boosts your confidence. But why should it always be the woman that is expected to do the cooking? Mum does, I am sorry to say; she's not at all the ideal role model. But I'm with Ali on this one, I think people should take turns. Tash agrees. She said rather pointedly to Ali, "*Take turns?* Right? Me and Emily have cooked!"

Ali by now was looking decidedly crushed, so I at once said that we would join in and help her as quite honestly I'm not sure she even knows how to boil an egg. As a result of all this, we are going to do a pie! A real proper pie, with real proper pastry. We're not doing it today, as we always go down to Auntie Jay's at the weekend, but tomorrow evening we intend to have a big cook-in. We're quite looking forward to it! Tash says it will be a three star entry in her food diary.

Monday

Huh! So much for a three star entry. The pie was a DISASTER! Well, actually, to be fair, it was the pastry that was a disaster. We can't blame Ali cos it was me and Tash that were responsible for it. We said that we would do the pastry if Ali took care of all the rest. Not that she had to do very much, just dump stuff in a pie dish. We were the real chefs!

I still don't actually know what went wrong. We looked up pastry in a cook book we borrowed from Auntie Jay, and we followed it *exactly*. I do have this sneaking feeling that maybe it shouldn't be bashed about quite as much as we bashed

it. Well, Tash more than me. She went at it like it was a punch ball – biff, boff, bam! She said she was "softening it". I then rolled it out *most carefully* with a bottle (cos we don't have a rolling pin) and was about to cut it into a suitable pie shape when Tash went and snatched it away from me and before I could stop her she had gone and scrunched it all up again and was wringing it out as if it were a wet tea towel. She said that it was "what you have to do".

I didn't argue with her, cos what do I know? I am not ashamed to admit that I know absolutely nothing. I can't help feeling it would be a rather nice gesture if Tash were now prepared to admit that she also knows absolutely nothing, but she obstinately insists that punching and pummelling is what you have to do. She says the only mistake we made was having two of us involved. "Too many cooks", etc. What she is obviously hinting at is that I must have rolled it out wrong. Well, whatever! If she wants to blame me, let her blame me. What do I care? As I said to her, "If it makes you feel happier."

Ali has been really good about it. She hasn't crowed, or said I told you so, which she easily could have done. She has always maintained that cooking simply isn't worth the effort. She would be quite happy just munching cheese sandwiches every night and gazing at pictures of exploding stars on the computer.

One thing we have decided: we are not going to attempt any more cooking!

Tuesday

It occurred to me this evening that being independent does have its drawbacks. There is just so much boring *drudgery*. Even though we have stopped cooking, for instance, there is still a huge great mound of washing-up in the sink. Where does it all come from???

Wednesday

School is the pits. Got D– for my geography homework and no mark at all for history. At the bottom of the page Miss Selby wrote "Did you really hope to get away with this?"

Just because I said that the thing Oliver Cromwell was most noted for was trashing churches and what distinguished the Cavaliers was that they wore long frilly knickers. Knickers is certainly what they look like, and no one can deny that Cromwell trashed churches, so what is her problem? She was most unpleasant about it. She is a most unpleasant sort of woman. I am just *so* fed up! Why can't we have boys?

I have come to the conclusion that single sex schools are not natural. It makes people cranky. (As witness Miss Selby. I bet she wouldn't be half so mean if we had boys.) Frankly I dread to think what havoc it's playing with our hormones. It will probably make us frigid and repressed. Not only that, people that go to mixed schools, which is *by far the majority*, have a simply massive great advantage. They get to have their pick before we're even allowed so much as a peek! Even when we do get a peek we are so overwhelmed at the sight of a Real Live Boy that we just go all coy and giggly and embarrass ourselves. It's just totally unfair!

I remarked upon this to Tash, and she agrees with me that it is unfair, likewise unnatural, but strongly denies that either of us has ever got coy or giggly. She says, "We are not coy or giggly sort of people. We are serious in our intent."

Well, wow! I asked her what intent she was talking about, and she said, "Boys, of course! What else?"

I moaned, "But we never get to meet any, and even when we do they turn out not to like girls!"

Tash told me quite sternly to pull myself together. She pointed out that next week is half term, when we are going down to Sidmouth to stay with Gran and Grandad. She said, "Who knows what we might find?"

I said, "What, in *Sidmouth*?" But on the whole I am feeling decidedly more cheerful this evening than I was earlier in the day. I think it's the prospect of just getting away for a bit, even if it's only to Sidmouth.

Thursday

We bumped into Gus on the way home this afternoon and I have gone all gooey. I feel like a big marshmallow! I thought I had got over all that, because after all, if a boy isn't into girls there is absolutely *no* point in tying yourself up in emotional knots,  but I just can't seem to help it!!! When he looks at me I turn to total mush. I go all squidgy! And when he smiles, with that cute little dimple thing in his chin, it makes me want to start screaming! Tash says it does exactly the same to her. She says, "It's like my insides are bathed in molten sunshine." Ooh! How poetic!

Needless to say, we behaved with *perfect propriety* when we were speaking to him. Like really cool! Well, you have to; there is such a thing as pride. We said hi, and smiled, and he said, "Oh… hi," and smiled back, and we walked up the road together, three abreast, with me in the middle, which I don't think pleased Tash too much as she did a bit of jostling, trying to usurp me, but I stood firm and didn't let her.

Gus said he was really sorry he couldn't make it on Saturday (meaning the Saturday of Avril's bash), and we both smiled like mad to show him that we don't bear grudges or hold it against him. In other words, it's quite OK, we understand, we are totally relaxed about such things. Which we are! But oh dear, it is *such* a waste.

As I said afterwards to Tash, "I still can't believe he doesn't fancy you!" She is so bright and bubbly, and so *pretty*, but not at all in a yucky way.

Tash said she couldn't believe that he didn't fancy me. "But we've done all we can. We've signalled our interest."

I know where she got *that* phrase! It was in last week's *Glam Girl* – "How to Signal your Interest."

Tash said, "If he hasn't picked up the signs, it can only mean one thing."

Actually, according to *Glam Girl*, it could mean all kinds of things. I said this to Tash. I said, "It could just mean that we're not his type."

"*Neither* of us?" shrieked Tash.

I don't mean to sound boastful, but I have to agree that that is not very likely. I mean, we are so completely different!

I was just dying to ask him why he couldn't make it on Saturday, but there is such a thing as being *too* obvious. I was kind of hoping that Tash might come blurting out with it, as it's the sort of thing she's prone to do. I waited, hopefully, but she just went on beaming and nodding and generally looking amiable – if a tad moronic, it has to be said. Being laid back doesn't suit Tash. She obviously took it to heart when I accused her a few weeks ago of being too upfront. I do hope I haven't cramped her style, because that would be a terrible thing to do to a person. Now I'm beginning to feel guilty! I could have cast a blight on her entire future love life. And thanks to me, we still have no idea what, *if anything*, Gus is doing next Saturday night, since it goes without saying that I wasn't bold enough to ask.

Oh, I shall be so glad when we can go down to Sidmouth and get away from all this terrifying complexity!

Friday

Hooray hurrah and three huge cheers! It is now officially HALF TERM and we're on holiday. We have packed all our stuff into one big suitcase, with a little set of wheels to drag it by as we are going down to Sidmouth by train. Well, we're getting the train from Swindon to Exeter, where Gran and Grandad are going to meet us, as Sidmouth has no railway station. It will be quite an adventure! We have always gone by car before. The good thing about going by train is that *you never know who you might end up sitting next to*. As Tash says, the possibilities are endless!

Week 5, Monday
Staying with Gran and Grandad is not what you would call madly exciting, but it is such a relief not having to rack our brains all the time, wondering what we are going to eat and whose turn it is to open the next tin! Added to which, Gran and Grandad are really lovely people and always so anxious for us to enjoy ourselves.

You might think, as they are *Dad's* parents, that Tash would be their favourite, but in fact it's Ali. I once heard Gran say to Mum that Ali is such "a sweet, old-fashioned sort of girl". Well, yuck, if anyone ever said that about me I would be seriously worried! Fortunately I don't think Ali heard, though even if she did it probably wouldn't bother her. She is truly someone who just doesn't seem to care a) what she looks like or b) what people think of her. Tash and I care like crazy! Gran and Grandad reckon we care too much. They say it is not right that girls of our age should be so fussed about their appearance and thinking all the time about *boys*. It seems that Gran didn't start thinking about boys until she was at least fifteen. Hm… what did she do all day? Play with her dolls?

Tuesday

Today we went to the Donkey Sanctuary. It's one of our favourite places to visit! We have now been there three times. The  donkeys are so sweet and friendly, they come niddy-nodding over to speak to you, and even Gran, who is not an animal person, cannot resist stroking them.

As well as looking at the donkeys, Tash and I were also on the look out for... you've guessed it! BOYS! We are always on the lookout for boys, but we didn't really see anything promising. Gran might actually be surprised to learn that we do in fact have our standards! We're not so desperate we would take just anything. Like most of them at the Donkey Sanctuary were way too young. Ten, eleven at most. I wouldn't want to hang out with a boy that was younger than me! No way. It seems, however, that older boys have no interest in donkeys, as we didn't spot a single one that was what might be termed "mature". I suppose they are all too busy playing football. Sigh. I don't mind football, but I do prefer donkeys!

Wednesday

Went to Exeter and looked round the shops. Found a charity shop selling second-hand clothes. Mostly junk,

but Tash got a rather snazzy top and I got a totally brilliant shirt. Ralph Lauren, in a heavenly bluey green.

Grandad couldn't understand why we should want to go and grub around in what he called "people's cast-offs". He said he would gladly buy us something new, but Gran told him that we had more than enough clothes – *as if* – and said the money would be better spent on books. "Of which they don't have anything like enough." Yeah yeah yeah! Books are OK, and I read as much as the next person, but you can get books from the library. You can't get clothes from the library! And what is this weird notion that you could possibly have *too many of them*?

Ali didn't buy anything to wear but she found a telescope, of all things, and the look on her face was just *so*, like, wistful, like really yearning, that

we nobly told Grandad to forget about buying us anything and just get Ali her heart's desire. I mean, really, it was *humongously* expensive, but I must say she is being very embarrassingly grateful, both to us and to Grandad. She says that a telescope is what she has always wanted.

It is nice to see Ali so happy.

Thursday

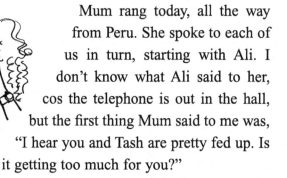

Mum rang today, all the way from Peru. She spoke to each of us in turn, starting with Ali. I don't know what Ali said to her, cos the telephone is out in the hall, but the first thing Mum said to me was, "I hear you and Tash are pretty fed up. Is it getting too much for you?"

I said no, of course it wasn't. The very idea! I was quite indignant. How could Ali even suggest such a thing? I told Mum that we *had* been a bit fed up last week, but more with school, and the general day-to-day struggle, and having to cope with unpleasant women such as Miss Selby. I said that now we were at Gran and Grandad's and being cosseted, we were feeling much better. I said, "It's like you, when you say you need a break."

Mum said, "Are you sure?" She was really anxious and all set to pack up and come whizzing back home. I screeched at her down the telephone, "*No!* We're managing perfectly OK." Mum still seemed doubtful, so when I handed over to Tash I told her to "Stand firm. Whatever you do! *Don't let her come rushing back.*"

Tash obviously followed my instructions cos Mum agreed in the end to stay put.

"I told her," said Tash, "we haven't burned the place down, we're not stuffing ourselves with junk food, and we're not having boys up there."

"Unfortunately," I said.

We both agreed, the chance would be a fine thing!

Friday

Started off by still feeling a bit sore with Ali, going and telling Mum we were fed up, but then we went down to the beach with Gran and Grandad and big surprise, miracle of miracles… *we have met a boy! A boy!!! In Sidmouth!* It is not the sort of place where you expect to meet anyone of either sex that is less than positively ancient.

How it happened, we were playing beach ball with Grandad. Grandad likes to play beach ball, as it makes him feel – I suppose – that he's still young. We think it only fair to humour him, since on the whole he is very good to us. It seems only kind. Gran just sits in her deck

chair and watches. She says she is "past all that kind of thing". Anyway, Grandad had thrown the ball, and Ali had missed it, and while she was still wondering where it had gone, me and Tash were racing off after it, and lo and behold, there he was... a real live boy! We almost, literally, bumped into him.

He is Spanish, and quite good looking. Must be at least fourteen. Maybe even fifteen. His name is Wackeen, or that's how he pronounces it. Seems a bit odd to me, but then I don't speak any Spanish, apart from "Ole, ole!" which makes him laugh. I wish I could snap my fingers! Wackeen can make his go off like gun shots, but mine just sound like stale cornflakes.

We were very puzzled about what he could be doing in a place like Sidmouth, but it seems he is staying with his sister, who is a waitress in one of the restaurants. Gran has promised that tomorrow, as it's our last night, we can go there for a meal, hooray!

I wish tomorrow *weren't* our last night. I wish we could have met Wackeen earlier. I wish we weren't going to spend all day driving to a place called Buckfast to see some stupid abbey. I don't want to see an abbey! I would rather see Wackeen! But Gran and Grandad have set their hearts on it. They just love going round old buildings, especially if they are holy. They would be really upset if I told them I didn't want to go.

What a lot of sacrificing one has to do in this life!

Have just broken off to discuss the situation with Tash. She informs me that I am the one Wackeen is attracted to; not her. I don't know whether this is true or not!!! He has a really beautiful smile, and I did notice that he seemed to take more notice of me than he did of Tash. If he really likes me better it must be because I have blonde hair. You probably don't get many people with blonde hair in Spain. Tash is being very good about it, I must say. She says she is really happy for me, and I believe her. I would be happy for her if it were the other way round!

Week 6, Saturday

I think Gran and Grandad really enjoyed their visit to the old abbey. I'm glad I didn't tell them that I'd rather have stayed behind and gone down to the beach; it would have been unkind. All the same, I couldn't help feeling it was a day wasted. I did quite like the abbey, but I would far rather have been with Wackeen!

Actually, I have now discovered that he is called Joaquin. Grandad laughed and laughed when I said Wackeen! Though to be honest, I couldn't really hear all that much difference; just a bit more huffing and puffing at the start, like Hhhho-ackeen. I'm sticking to Wackeen!

We saw him this evening in his sister's restaurant. They were really busy and he was helping out, so we didn't get much of a chance to talk. But he kept catching my eye across the room and winking at me, and I kept dissolving into giggles, mainly because Tash would

keep *prodding* and *nudging*. Ali didn't get what was happening, she kept going, "What? What is it?" and Gran told me in reproving tones to "Stop being so obvious, Emily! It's demeaning." Well, ho! I bet Gran was obvious enough in her day, even if she didn't start till she was fifteen. I've seen photos of her in mini skirts!

Tomorrow we have to go back home. I do wish we didn't. It is *so* frustrating. Just as I've met someone! If I could just have one more day I feel that Wackeen and me could really get to know each other. Tash is right, it *is* me he goes for. He is definitely interested! But he is going home himself tomorrow, so no chance. He has promised that he will write to me, so I am trying to be hopeful, but I have read too often in magazines like *Glam Girl* about holiday romances which come to nothing. Tash has done her best to cheer me up by pointing out that living in Spain "he wouldn't actually be much *use* to you. Like you couldn't take him to parties, or anything."

I know she is right, but I could at least tell everyone that I had a boyfriend, and show them pictures. Tash says I could still do that, if I wanted. We got Grandad to take loads of photos in the restaurant, and Tash swears she would never give me away.

"I'd never tell anyone he wasn't really your boyfriend."

That is so sweet of her! But I think it would be just too sad to pretend that someone was my boyfriend when he wasn't. I said this to Tash, and reluctantly she agreed with me. She said, "It's a nice idea, but you're right. The time for fantasy is over! What we need are *real* boys."

I mean, for goodness' sake, we are nearly thirteen!

Sunday

Back home. Back to buying toilet rolls and thinking what to eat. Back to *independent living*!!!

To make matters worse, it's my turn to do the cooking! Except that I have decided Ali is right, and that tins are the way to go. Went shopping after we got back and now the cupboard is positively bursting. Hooray! A tin a day keeps hunger away. And, as Tash says, will keep us going if the terrorists come. She is still obsessed!

Earlier, coming back from the station in a cab (Grandad gave us the money! He is so sweet), we arrived home at the same moment as Gus. I had forgotten how beautiful he is. On a scale of one to ten I would give Wackeen about... mm... six. Maybe seven. But Gus I would give 9.9999999!

And he is so polite, as well. He actually carried our suitcase up the stairs for us! Needless to say we invited him in, but he wouldn't come. He pointed at our BOYS BEWARE sign on the door and said, "I don't think so!"

Tash said, "Oh, *that*. You don't want to take any notice of *that*," and immediately ripped it off; but he still wouldn't come in. He said that he had "things to catch up on".

Ali, meanwhile, had gone down to the basement to collect Fat Man, who has been looked after by Auntie Jay. She was down there for such a long time that Tash and I almost forgot about her. Ali just seems incapable of ever doing anything at normal speed. Then when she finally put in an appearance… no Fat Man! Auntie Jay wasn't there, she said; she must be at the shops.

Tash said, "It's taken you all this time to find out?" Ali said no, she had been talking to Gus. "About what?" said Tash.

Eagerly Ali said, "I was telling him about my telescope!"

Tash and I exchanged glances. We could just imagine Ali going on in that way that she does. You don't get a word out of her for hours on end, then all of a sudden she gets a bee in her bonnet and there's no stopping her. I just hope she didn't bore the poor boy rigid.

Week 6, Monday
Back at school. It's not actually too bad; even Miss Selby seems to be in a bit of a better mood than she was. I passed her in the upper corridor this morning and she

stretched her lips at me. Tash said it was a smile. More like a grimace, I would have thought, but maybe it's the best she can do. After all these years of being pursed together in a thin line, her lip muscles have probably got paralysed.

Everyone in our class was full of stories about what they had done over half term. Loads of people claimed to have met BOYS. Boys by the bucketful! Avril Mackie, in particular. She always claims to have met boys, but I have noticed that there never seems to be any kind of *proof*. I shall have proof! As soon as Grandad sends the photos. Tash seemed really eager to tell everyone about Wackeen, so I just sat back and let her get on with it. I heard her say, "It was Emily he fancied! He was all over her!"

Meg, Shauna and the others were dead impressed. I could tell from the way they were looking at me, like, "Wow!" Like seeing me through new eyes. I mean, the fact that *Tash* said he fancied me! Obviously if I'd said it, it would have been more like polite smiles and "Oh, yeah?"

It makes you feel good when your friends look at you with respect. And it is all thanks to Tash! It's lovely that we are so loyal to each other.

Tuesday

Discussed Miss Selby over tea. (Spaghetti hoops and mashed bananas.) I speculated that the reason she is so sour and embittered is that she has never managed to get herself a man. Tash agreed that that might be the case, but then suggested that possibly she was sour and embittered to begin with, and thus no man will go anywhere near her. She added that of course she might be a lesbian. I said, "Not that that is any reason to be sour and embittered because look at Auntie Jay… she is anything *but* sour and embittered."

At this point, somewhat to our surprise as we didn't think she had been paying any attention, Ali joined in and told us that we were talking nonsense. She said, "Auntie Jay isn't a lesbian."

Well, pardon me, but how does she know? She might be some kind of expert on astrology, or astronomy, or whatever it is, but when it comes to matters of s.e.x. she knows next to nothing at all!

Tash explained – quite nicely and gently – that just because one doesn't like the idea of something, doesn't mean it isn't true.

"And in any case," I said, "there is nothing *wrong* with being a lesbian."

By now Ali had gone that dull sort of red which is what always happens when she's bottling things up. Unlike me and Tash, who let it all hang out (or so Mum says), Ali is a bottler. We tried to encourage her. We told her to "Say it, whatever it is," but she wouldn't. She just muttered again that we were talking nonsense and went off to her broom cupboard, scooping Fat Man into her arms as she went.

111

Ali is *such* a puzzle! There is simply no understanding her.

Wednesday

Me and Tash are really angry. Really *really* angry. Ali has absolutely gone and done it! Yesterday, we felt fond of her. Today we are *seething*. We'd like to lock her in her cupboard and leave her there. She is not fit to be let out!

It just so happened that we both stayed late after school, me for the drama club and Tash for tennis practice. We didn't get back till half-past five, by which time…

Suffice it to say that Ali has been up to her old tricks. *Talking* to people. People she finds on the street. People that drink, and stink, and probably take drugs. People you wouldn't want to be within a million miles of! And there was one of them, sitting in *our room*, at *our table*, eating *our food*.

Me and Tash nearly went ballistic! I really thought that Ali had grown out of that disgusting habit. It is so unwholesome, and she is just so *totally indiscriminate*. She sees these people sitting there, in shop doorways, and she starts up these mad conversations, and next thing you know she's claiming they're her friend, and bringing them back home to stink the place out. Cos this one did stink! We could smell it as soon as we opened the door. I don't mean to be unsympathetic, but it was just, like, completely and utterly DISGUSTING. Only of course you can't actually say anything, since you don't want to hurt people's feelings.

Ali, as usual, remained blissfully unaware. She has this ability, things just wash over her. All bright and happy she tells us that this is Patricia, who's just popped in for a bite to eat. Patricia looks like a pickled walnut, and I can't decide whether it's dirt or suntan. She's also raving bonkers. Mum wouldn't like me saying that as she is all for tolerance, but it just happens to be *true*. We got rid of her double quick and immediately scrubbed the table with Dettol. We are just so furious! We have both laid into Ali, telling her it will be all her fault if we go down with some dread disease or get eaten alive by fleas.

I said, "You can't do things like that! It's irresponsible."

"It's dangerous," said Tash. "You could have got us all *murdered*."

Well, she could! Patricia was definitely certifiable. We said this – well, shouted it, actually – and Ali just sat there, like completely unmoved. She wasn't bottling: we just weren't getting through to her. She waited till we'd finished yelling, then calmly stood up and said, "She can't help the way she is, she's had a very hard life." And that was that! End of conversation.

Oh, God, Ali is so so weird! Did she do this thing to pay us back for upsetting her yesterday? Saying about Auntie Jay being a lesbian? Or did it just suddenly come over her, that she had to bring this stinking old woman back home? Mum once said that Ali has a "good heart", and I know – I know! – that people like Patricia are lost souls and cannot help the way they are, I know that Ali is right and I am wrong, but it is very difficult to bear!

Thursday

Tash says she has been bitten by a flea. It could have come off Fat Man – or it could have come off Patricia. We are still *very cross* with Ali. We have told her, it is good to have compassion, but there is a limit. Unfortunately, I don't think Ali knows what limits are. It's like she has to watch *Star Trek* every day. I mean, *every single day*. We think she is probably a lost cause.

Gran rang up this evening to tell us that the photographs are on the way. Hurrah! I am longing to see them.

Friday

The photographs have come and they are great of Wackeen but not so good of me. Well, I don't think they are. I think they make me look lumpy. I said this to Tash and she told me that I was talking rubbish. She said, "Nothing could make you look lumpy, you're far too slim."

I said, "But my face looks fat! Look at it!"

Tash looked and said she couldn't see anything wrong with my face, and she took the photographs to school with her and insisted on showing them to everyone.

I kept trying to stop her. I screeched, "No, don't! They're horrible!" But people just kept snatching and grabbing and passing them round.

Actually, I don't think they're *too* bad. Of me, I mean. It's only one that makes me look lumpy. The rest are quite good, I might even take them into Boots and get them blown up, except maybe that would be a bit show-offy. It's not like I'm a movie star, or anything! But there is one of me and Wackeen together that I specially like. Everyone was going "Ooh" and "Aah" as they looked at it. I wonder if he will ever write to me???

Avril said it was a pity I couldn't bring him along tomorrow as we are going to be very short of boys, so then we had to break the bad news about Gus not coming. Everyone was hugely disappointed, it made us feel like we had let them down. Kim said, "Well! I thought by now you'd have managed to get somewhere." We found this remark somewhat irritating. Like she thought *she* would have got anywhere!

Tash, with great dignity, said, "It just so happens that he's not into girls."

There was this sort of silence, then Ishara, who is still quite babyish, said, "How can you tell?"

Tash said, "You just can."

"Like if he doesn't fancy *Tash*," I said.

"And he doesn't fancy Em—"

"He could still come along," said Kim.

But we cannot face another brush off! It would be too humiliating. We quickly changed the subject and told them instead about Ali and how she had brought this old woman all covered in fleas back home with her. Everyone immediately screeched out in horror: "Ugh! Fleas!"

I said, "Yes, it was foul, but that's Ali for you."

Kim said, "Gross!"

Zoella wanted to know if Ali had got herself a boyfriend yet, and me and Tash gave these hollow laughs, like ho-ho-ho, but without any chuckle in the middle. I said this was what worried us. "How will she *ever* get one? She never goes anywhere, she never does anything!"

Zoella then said that she had this great idea. She said her cousin William is staying with them over the weekend. She said he's fifteen and "quite nice" and "hugely clever" but kind of "not very good-looking, if you know what I mean?" She says he finds it difficult to get girlfriends, being a bit shy as well as not very good-looking. She said, "He'd be just right for Ali!"

Tash and I agreed that he sounded like Ali's sort of person, and Avril has said it's OK if they both come along, so now we are really hopeful that we may have found a boyfriend for her. Tash says they will be able to sit together and be as clever as they like.

I said, "Yes, they can spend all evening talking to each other about red midgets and exploding holes and black whatever they ares." And it won't matter if Ali refuses to get dressed up or let us fix her hair, cos William won't be fashion conscious and he probably won't even notice that she chews her nails, and she won't mind that he's not good-looking cos they'll both be far too busy talking boffin talk.

It will be such a relief if we can get Ali set up! It will be a weight off our minds. It will mean that we can concentrate all our energies on ourselves, for a change. I think Mum will be pleased too, cos I know she worries about Ali. Tash says we should have done it ages ago. "Found a boy for Ali." She says Ali will be so much happier being *normal*. I agree! It can't be nice to always feel that you are an outsider.

She is not here at the moment, but as soon as she comes in we are going to tell her. She has a date!

MATCHMAKERS UNITED!!!

Week 7, Saturday

Well. So much for trying to help people. Talk about ingratitude! Ali rolled up at six o'clock and we immediately told her about the invitation – the very *kind and thoughtful* invitation, considering she isn't even one of us – and she said, "Oh, but I can't, I'm doing things."

Quite frankly, we were staggered. When does Ali ever do things? I mean, *real* things. Going-out-in-a-group-and-having-fun-type things. She doesn't! Not ever.

Tash said, "When you say *things*—"

Ali said, "I've got stuff arranged."

I said, "What *stuff*?"

"Stuff," said Ali.

She is always so vague! She is for ever drifting in and out and not saying where she has been or who she has been there with. It's useless to ask her as she will never tell you. I guess she's going round to see Louise; she is the only friend we've ever heard her talk about. Goodness only knows what they get up to! Me and Tash grew quite impatient. Tash said, "If it's Louise, you see her all the time. Surely just for once you could do something different?"

I told her that Avril had invited her specially. "Zoella's cousin is coming. He's a real egghead!" (Dad's way of saying boffin.) "He's desperate to meet you." Tash added that they would find "so much to talk about." But Ali just dug in her heels and said again that she had "stuff arranged". She is a truly maddening person! She is just *so* stubborn.

We spent half the evening lecturing her. We said, "It's for your own good." We came straight out with it, we told

her: "You'll never get a boyfriend if you carry on like this!" We told her that she didn't know how to speak to boys, or how to behave with boys. We told her how she didn't take enough care about the way she dressed or the way she looked. We said, "You have to make an effort. These things don't happen all on their own." We may have seemed a bit brutal, but sometimes I do believe you have to be cruel to be kind. She cannot go on the way she is!!!

She sat in silence as we talked, but I honestly don't know how much she took in. You can never tell with Ali whether she is actually listening to you or whether she is wandering off some place else. In her mind, I mean. At the end, when we'd exhausted ourselves and couldn't think of a single other thing to say, she still just went on sitting there. I said, "Ali, we're not getting at you! It's just that we worry."

She said, "Yes, I know. I must go and do my homework now." And disappeared into her broom cupboard!

Tash and I are agreed: that is the *very last time* we bother. There are some people who just refuse to be helped, and Ali is obviously one of them.

I am now going to get ready, as we are leaving in half an hour. I don't know what Ali is up to, and I really don't care. I just feel sorry for poor William. He is going to be so disappointed!

Saturday. Evening.

Well, talk about a let down! Talk about birthday *bash*. It wasn't a bash at all! Avril's mum and dad were there. *And* her granny. *And* one of her aunties. Tash said it was more like an old folks' convention! And not a single solitary boy except for Avril's brother, who is too nerdy to count, and Zoella's cousin William. Who is also nerdy. But the hugest of boffins!

I tried talking to him, just out of politeness, really, and also because nobody else was bothering, plus I felt kind of responsible, what with Ali not turning up, so I made this big effort and after about five minutes I felt like my brain was glazing over. I just don't know *how* we got on to quadratic equations. It's hardly what you would call a normal subject for conversation, though Ali might have found it so. I daresay she would enjoy talking about quadratic equations. She would find it stimulating. I'm sure people that are into them just love to exchange quadratic equation-type gossip. They might even make jokes! Me, I nearly died of boredom. It probably didn't help that I can't actually remember what a quadratic equation *is*.

Fortunately I can report that the evening was not a total waste as there was a gorgeous Orlando Bloom look-alike waiting tables. *Our* table. We all fancied him like crazy! He, however, had eyes for no one but Tash. He kept ogling her, and she kept ogling back. If Gran thought I was being obvious with Wackeen, she should have seen Tash playing up to Orlando! Kim was really put out. She kept swizzling round on her chair and

flashing these big lighthouse beams at him, but he took
no notice, and serve her right. Personally I would never
humiliate myself like that, I think it is truly demeaning.

Tash, needless to say, has now gone all obsessive and
can't stop talking about it. I don't begrudge her her little
moment of triumph. Far from it. I am happy for her! She
deserves it; after all, it was her turn. It would have been
just *too* embarrassing if it had been me he had gone for!

It is now half-past nine and Ali has come strolling in.
We have very pointedly not asked her where she has
been, but we do think, if *we* have to be home by half-
past eight, then so should she. I know she is older than
me and Tash, but she is not in the least bit streetwise. I
am surprised at Auntie Jay, letting her stay out so late. I
also think it was quite mean of her – Ali, that is – not to

have come with us tonight. We *told* her that William was going to be there. They would have got on so well together! I said to her that he was really disappointed not to meet her. I said, "He is such an intelligent person... he told me all about quadratic equations." I thought Ali would be impressed. I mean, she knows about these things! But all she said was, "That's an odd thing to talk about." and went into her broom cupboard.

She is the odd one, if you ask me. She will never get a boyfriend if she carries on like this.

If it hadn't been for Orlando Bloom the evening would have been a bit of a let down. We have been trying to think what else we have to look forward to. There is Shauna's party in two weeks' time. Maybe that will live up to expectations.

Sunday

I do truly begin to wonder whether I will ever bother getting married, because I simply couldn't *stand* having to go shopping every week, and do cooking and

 housework all the time. Tash says the answer is to a) find a partner that is rich rich RICH or b) pursue a

career that pays LOADSAMONEY. That is all very well, but I have recently been thinking that I might like to work with donkeys, like at the Donkey Sanctuary, for example, and I don't think that that would pay loadsamoney. Plus I would probably want to marry someone who also worked with donkeys, so that we could indulge our donkey passion together, and that means we wouldn't have a bean between us and

then it would be nothing but drudgery. Why is life so complicated???

Tash has asked Auntie Jay if we can all go and eat in the pizza restaurant next Saturday. She said, "They do such heavenly gorgeous pizzas!" (Meaning: they have such heavenly gorgeous waiters.) Auntie Jay has said why not, what a good idea. I didn't tell her that Tash just wants to make eyes at Orlando Bloom!

Monday

I bought a copy of *Glam Girl* on the way in to school. Tash likes *Teens*, I like *Glam Girl*. Mrs McDonald, on the other hand, doesn't like either!!! It was one of the first things she told us when we moved up to Year 8. She said, "Gurrrls!" which made us nearly leap out of our skins as we thought she was having a fit, or something. It's just the way she talks. She sounds like a machine gun with a frog in its throat. "I have tae tell ye, gurrls, that I will *nae* tolerrrate trrrash in ma classrrroom!" By trash she means virtually every magazine you can think of plus "pink books in shiny covers", in other words, exactly the kind of books we all like to read! Shopping 'n snogging 'n a soupspoon of s-s-s-sex... Mrs McDonald says she "cannae abide them". She gave us "due warrrning".

"If I catch so much as a glimpse o' one, I will tek it off ye!"

She is always tekking them off us. She may be old, but boy, she has eyes like laser beams! Not to mention a nose like a bloodhound. I swear she can sniff things out! Fortunately our first period was geography, with Mr Askew, who didn't even notice when Tash one day had a nose bleed all over her desk, so I was able to sit there undisturbed reading this *extremely* interesting article on "How to Make the Most of Yourself". Which, in my humble opinion, is likely to be of far more use to me in life than learning about rift valleys.

I told Tash about it at break, so then she wanted to borrow the magazine and read it in the next lesson, which was history, but I wouldn't let her cos if Mrs McDonald has eyes like lasers, Miss Selby has ones that come out on stalks. They do! They are spring-loaded. They suddenly shoot out from the  front of the class and land in front of you, *whoosh! donk!* when you are least expecting it. Very off-putting to find these baleful eyes suddenly glaring up at you. Tash sulked a bit, but I let her have a read over lunch and now we are eagerly thinking up new ways to make the most of ourselves ready for Shauna's party, which is bound to be good as her parties always are.

Tuesday

Didn't get much sleep last night. We had been in bed for about an hour, and Tash was happily snoring (which she said she wasn't, but how would she know?) when I heard this strange sound, like a sort of... swishing. Slithering. I opened my eyes to see a white shape moving across the room, dragging something behind it. I said, "*Ali?*"

Tash then gave this enormous snore and woke herself up and said, "Wozzappnin?" I switched on the light and we saw Ali, trailing her duvet cover.

I shrieked, "What are you doing?" I mean, it was practically the middle of the night.

Ali said, "This duvet cover *smells*."

Well! I'm surprised she even noticed. Tash muttered somewhat sourly that Patricia had probably sat on it. I suggested that maybe Fat Man had had an accident. Ali said, "It's nothing to do with Fat Man. It's just been on the bed too long. I expect yours smells, too." So we picked it up and sniffed it, and omigod she was right! It was *putrid*. So then we sniffed the sheet and the pillows, and they were putrid, as well.

Tash said, "How long have we been here?"

I unlocked my diary and looked it up. I said, "Six weeks."

Tash said it was no wonder they stank. "We should have changed them ages ago. Mum does it every week!"

More work. But actually it was quite fun as we decided to have a wash-in and we stuffed both the sheets and all the pillow cases in the machine, and re-made the beds, and had a cup of tea and sat round drinking it and cosily chatting, which is something we hardly ever do. Well, not all three of us together. Certainly not at

midnight! It was good that we did cos it made us fond of Ali all over again. We talked about boys (among other things) and Tash said she hoped Ali didn't think we'd been getting at her the other day, when we lectured her. She said, "We worry about you." Ali admitted that most of the girls in her class have boyfriends and that they all think she is peculiar. I suddenly felt this strong kind of protective thing. I said heatedly that that wasn't fair. I said, "You're far cleverer than any of them are!"

Tash added that she could be far prettier than any of them, as well, if she just took a bit more trouble. She said, "You can still be clever! Being clever doesn't mean you can't make the best of yourself."

We then had this long, intense, girly discussion about what Ali could do to improve herself, with me and Tash offering advice from all our years of experience. As we pointed out, Ali is just starting: we have been at it for ever! Well, since we were about ten, I suppose. I think Ali was grateful. At any rate she listened to what we had to say and she seemed to take it all in. Now perhaps we shall see some improvement!

I was quite tired this morning and found it hard to wake up, but now I seem to have got my second wind. I enjoyed last night's session! I am so pleased that we have been able to help Ali.

Wednesday

Something so weird! In the middle of the night, bombs started exploding. Me and Tash shot out of bed in a panic. We thought it was terrorists! I crashed into the table, and Tash stubbed her toe against a chair and screamed, at the top of her voice, at which point Ali came rushing out of her broom cupboard going, "What is it, what is it?"

Tash shrieked, "We're under attack!" and clutched at me with both hands. Then I clutched at her and we both shrieked together. I mean, it was really scary!

Ali said, "It's somewhere in the room."

Whatever it was, it was still going off. *Bang. Crack! Fizz. Pop! Bang.* Like fireworks, except that it seemed to be coming from the food cupboard, where we keep all the tins. I moaned, "They've planted something!"

Tash yelled at Ali to "Keep away!"

I don't know whether Ali is brave or just foolhardy. Me and Tash were already halfway to the door. We implored her to "Get out, get out!" The cupboard was still exploding; quite honestly, we thought the whole thing was going to go. We crouched there, ready to run for our lives. I am not ashamed to say this! I think self-preservation is a duty. After all, how would Mum and Dad feel if we got blown up? I screeched, "Ali! Leave it!" But she wouldn't. She just had to go and look. We watched, shaking like jellies, while Ali went on tiptoe 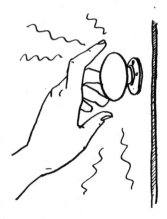 across the room and ever so, ever so slowly reached out a hand and... opened... the... cupboard... door...

Grapefruit. It was grapefruit! A mouldy old cereal bowl, full of exploding grapefruit!

Ali, in disgusted tones, said, "This must have been here for weeks! When did anyone last eat grapefruit?"

Sheepishly, as we edged back into the room, Tash said, "That was the day we were going to be late for school and I didn't have time to finish breakfast."

I said, "You mean that day when we'd already been late the day before?"

"Yes, and Miss Selby caught us trying to sneak in and almost went ballistic."

I couldn't believe it. I said, "That was way back before half term!"

Tash said, "Yes, I know. I shoved it in the cupboard and forgot all about it."

We were standing there, watching the grapefruit as it fizzed and popped, when there was a knock at the door. It was Gus! Oh, dear, so embarrassing! We were in our nighties!!! He seemed as embarrassed as we were. He gave this little smile, like sort of half bewildered and half apologetic, and said, "What's happening?"

Tash assured him, in her brightest and breeziest tones, that it was quite all right. "Just a few problems with a grapefruit."

I giggled and said, "It's exploding!"

I guess this confused him even more. He said, "Exploding?" Like he had never heard of such a thing. (Well, who has?)

I said, "Oh, yes, they explode all the time, you know."

Ali, picking up the bowl, said, "Only if people put them in cupboards and forget them." She held out the bowl for Gus to see. "It's been there so long it's fermenting."

Gus peered at it and said, "Way out!" I think he was quite impressed. I was impressed! I had no idea that grapefruits could turn themselves into bombs. Upon reflection, this is probably how most of the world's great discoveries have been made i.e. *by accident*.

Gus said, "Dangerous stuff! Doesn't exactly make you feel like eating grapefruit again, does it?" He then added something which I thought was truly witty. He said, "Kind of gives a whole new meaning to grapefruit cocktail."

And then he said goodnight and went back downstairs, and *we let him go*. Why didn't we ask him in??? I know it was three o'clock in the morning, but we could all have cosily sat round with cups of tea, like we did the night before. We might have got to know him properly at last. Oh, I do wish we had! He looked so cute in his dressing gown and pyjamas. It's not like me and Tash to be slow on the uptake, we are usually alert for every opportunity. (Like it says in *Glam Girl*: WAIT, WATCH AND POUNCE!)

"I thought it was – you know!" Tash looked a bit shamefaced. "Terrorists." I had to admit that so did I. Of course it all seems funny *now* – now that we know what it really was. But to be woken up in the middle of the night by guns going off is actually quite frightening, and has made us far more in sympathy with all those poor people that live in places where it happens the whole time.

We sat there, gravely discussing it, while Ali cleared up the mess. I said, "You're our bomb disposal expert!" which made Tash giggle.

Ali said, "I'm glad you find it amusing."

"Well, you must admit," I said, "grapefruit cocktail…"

Tash giggled again. Ali glared.

I said, "What? What's the matter?"

Tash said, "What have we done now?"

Ali snapped that it was what we hadn't done that was the matter. "You didn't either of you care about Fat Man!"

It took us a second or so to get over our surprise. I mean, Ali almost never snaps. Tash was the first to recover. As Ali disappeared into her broom cupboard she yelled, "I didn't notice you caring that much, either!"

Ali stuck her head back round the door. "*I* knew it wasn't gunfire," she said.

Tash said, "How? How could you possibly know that?"

Ali gave us this really pitying look. "Why would anyone be sitting in our food cupboard firing a gun?"

Tash, blustering a bit, said, "Well, they could have been hiding."

"Not in our food cupboard," said Ali.

Tash and I are agreed, Ali simply has *no* imagination.

Thursday

Today I fell asleep in PSE. I was just so-o-o tired. Unfortunately, it is Miss Selby who is taking us for PSE this term. Wouldn't you know it! Dear Mrs Meek was so woffly and woolly, she probably wouldn't even have noticed. But the old spring-loaded eyes came shooting out and spotted me. I wasn't even snoring! Just sitting there, quite quietly, snoozing in the corner and not disturbing a soul.

Miss Selby was most unpleasant. As usual. Tash tried valiantly to come to my rescue. She said, "Excuse me, but it's not Emily's fault. We haven't had much sleep just lately." She then went on to explain, in some detail, all about exploding grapefruits, and gunmen in the food cupboard, and people rushing upstairs in droves. I must admit, she did go on rather, but that is just Tash, she gets carried away. There was absolutely no reason for Miss Selby to tell her to "Stop this inane burble." I thought that was really rude. Really uncalled for.

Miss Selby is obviously psychotic, and I don't believe that she was smiling at me the other day, when she stretched her lips. I think she was trying to bare her teeth, like, "You just watch it, Emily Love! I'm going to get you."

I wish someone would get *her*. Maybe one day she'll drive herself completely mad and they'll lock her up. And a good job, too! The world would be a safer place without her.

Friday

When we went downstairs this morning, there was a postcard waiting for us on the hall table. My heart leaped – my knees went wobbly – I broke into a sweat. The classic symptoms of Lovesick Anticipation. (There was an article about it in *Glam Girl*.) My one thought was, "Wackeen!"

Tash, needless to say, went barging ahead and snatched it up before I could get there. "Ooh," she goes, "who's this from?"

I yelled, "Gimme, gimme!"

Tash said, "Why?"

I wailed, "Oh, Tash, lemme have it!"

So she did, but it was from Mum and Dad. I am, naturally, very happy to have a card from Mum and Dad

– well, actually, it was to all of us – but I do begin to wonder if I shall *ever* hear from Wackeen. I can't write to him as I don't have his address. But I gave him mine, and he promised faithfully that he would keep in touch.

I said to Tash, as we walked up the road to the bus stop, that I thought I would have to reconcile myself to the fact that it had obviously been one of those intense holiday romances which fizzle away to nothing once the holiday is over. Tash – *stupidly* – giggled and said, "Intense? You only knew him for two days!" Ali, who was with us, also giggled. What right Ali has to giggle, I really do not know, considering she must come *way* up the top of the list of World's Most Ignorant People. In matters of personal relationships, that is. Has she ever had a holiday romance? No! Has she ever had a boyfriend? No! Is she ever likely to get a boyfriend? No! Not unless she starts to pay a bit more attention to the things that matter.

She doesn't even know any boys! She has absolutely no idea what interests them, or how to talk to them. And there she was, daring to snigger at *me*!

They could obviously tell that they had upset me. They both apologised, sounding quite contrite. I was just starting to unruffle myself and feel calm again when Tash had to go and point out that "You didn't actually properly know him, though, did you?" Some people just always have to have the last word. Except that I didn't let her!

A bit snappishly I said, "Do you actually properly know Orlando?" (Which is how we have been referring to the Orlando Bloom look-alike in the pizza restaurant.) Tash had to admit that she didn't. Ali then wanted to know who Orlando was. I said, "Orlando Bloom, and Tash has been mooning over him for the past week. *Haven't* you?" Tash nodded; very pink and excited. At the mere mention of him, she'd gone all gooey, like a big sticky meringue. Triumphantly, I said, "Well, there you are, then! And you've never even spoken to him… you don't even know his name!"

Ali, sounding puzzled, said, "I thought you said it was Orlando Bloom?"

I said, "He *looks* like Orlando Bloom… which is why she's gone all gushy!"

Tash moaned, happily. Ali said, "But who is he?"

I told her that he was a waiter in the restaurant we are

going to tomorrow evening with Auntie Jay. Ali said, "What, Orlando Bloom? He's a waiter?"

I said, "No, his look-alike!"

Ali said, "Oh." And then she thought about it a bit and said, "So who *is* this Orlando Bloom guy?"

It is unbelievable. Tash howled, "Gimme a break!"

I said, "Ali, you have to get your act together!"

Ali said, "But who *is* he?"

We explained that he was "just some actor that everybody in the world has heard of except you."

Tash added that, "There is life outside of *Star Trek*, you know."

It just goes to confirm what I said a few minutes ago about Ali being top of the list when it comes to ignorance. She must be about the only person alive that hasn't heard of Orlando Bloom! Well, apart from a few odd folk that live under stones or at the North Pole. I guess she felt our disapproval as she deliberately stayed downstairs on the bus while we went on top. Tash was

 all of a fizz and a bubble at the thought of seeing the Beloved tomorrow night. She confessed to me that even if you don't "actually properly" know someone, you can still have "extremely intense" feelings about them, and she said she shouldn't have laughed about me and Wackeen. Of

course I said that I forgave her, and within seconds we were the best of friends again.

It is such a comfort to have someone like Tash, knowing that you can confide in each other and tell each other things that you wouldn't tell another living soul. I could never confide in Ali the way I can confide in Tash; Ali just wouldn't understand. I couldn't even confide in Meg or Zoella. They would probably understand, but I would be just too embarrassed. With Tash and me, there are no secrets. We discussed our feelings for Wackeen and Orlando all the way to school. It was very satisfying.

At break, Kim showed us some special stuff she had got which sprays gold dust over your hair. Tash is now determined to go into town first thing tomorrow morning and buy some. It's rather expensive, in fact it is *outrageously* expensive, but I guess nothing is too good for Orlando!

Week 8, Saturday

Tash has bought her gold dust and sprayed it in her hair. I have told her that it looks *très sophistiqué*. It ought to, the amount it cost! But Tash is happy, and that is what counts. She says there is a whole range of colours, including emerald, which she thinks would suit me. I may perhaps get some for Shauna's party, but it's not worth splashing out just for going to the pizza restaurant with Auntie Jay. I don't remember noticing any other famous look-alikes waiting table! In any case, it is Tash's evening and I wouldn't want to spoil it for her by trying to compete.

Tash has just emerged from the bathroom and given me a twirl. She looks stunning! She's wearing a stripy vest top, black and gold, with her black skirt that Mum always says is too short, and cowboy boots like you sometimes see Madonna wearing. Plus, of course, the *very expensive* gold dust in her hair. If Orlando has any taste at all, he will take one look at her and that will be it. Wow! Smitten! I've told her this and she has gone a bit pink and said, "D'you reckon?" She seemed anxious about something. It's only now that I have noticed... she's gone and sprayed gold dust on her eyelids! It's kind of stuck on to her eye make-up, which is what I would call green but she says it's "aqua". Green is naff, aqua is cool. She's obviously not quite sure about it, though, cos she has just asked me whether I don't think it's a bit too *bling*? I have assured her that it isn't. But I have told her that she will have to keep blinking, and batting her eyelids, if she wants Orlando to get the full effect. So now she has gone back into the bathroom to practise.

I am not wearing anything special as I think it would be unfair to Tash; well, on this particular occasion. Not when we go to Shauna's party! Then it will be no holds barred!!! But today I have just got on an old top and a pair of washed-out jeans. I think—

Goodness! Ali has just appeared. She has really taken our lecture to heart. She has pulled her hair back, tight, into a pony tail, so that it's all lovely and swishy, and she has actually put on some lipstick and eye shadow. *Ali!* It is amazing what a difference it makes. She is also wearing a pair of trousers that I swear I have never seen before, with a shirt and a waistcoat that I didn't even know she had. Can she have sneaked out and bought them without telling us? It's just the sort of thing she would do!

Tash has re-emerged from the bathroom and her jaw has dropped open. She is every bit as knocked out as I am! We have both assured Ali that she looks "really nice" and I can see that she's pleased to have our approval. I'm thinking to myself, however (though I am certainly not saying so to Ali) that it's a bit excessive to go to all this trouble just to sit in a restaurant and eat pizza with Auntie Jay, and me and Tash. Unless maybe she thinks there are likely to be more Orlando Blooms hanging around? If that is the case, I'm afraid she is going to be disappointed, but it is a good start and it would not do to discourage her.

I am now the only one who is not dressed up! I could always go and change, but there doesn't seem much point. I remember all the other waiters as being quite boring. Some of them were really old. So I am going to stay as I am and be the Ugly Sister!

Sunday

I do *so* wish that Ali would learn to communicate. It wasn't just us and Auntie Jay that went for a meal last night. Gus and his dad came, as well!!! And Ali *knew* about it. All the time, she knew about it! She wasn't in the least bit surprised to see them waiting there, when we went downstairs to meet Auntie Jay. We were! Me and Tash had absolutely no idea they were coming with us. And there was me, looking like the Ugly Sister, and Tash and Ali all dressed up, gnash gnash, much grinding of teeth. Ali dressed up, and me dressed down! I looked such a sight, I just wanted to *die*.

Jo came with us too, and as there wasn't room for us

all to squeeze into one car Auntie Jay said that somebody would have to go with Gus and his dad. Normally I'd have seized the opportunity. I would have been in there just *sooo* fast. There would have been no stopping me! But last night I was just, like, too shaken for seizing opportunities. Too demoralised. Well, I mean, I wasn't dressed for it. I felt so dowdy! I felt so *plain*. Tash, on the other hand, being all glammed up and oozing confidence through every pore, was practically halfway in before Auntie Jay managed to haul her back out. She said, "Ali! You go."

Tash was not best pleased, I could tell. In fact she tried to cram herself in after Ali, but Auntie Jay just hauled her out again. She said, "You two come with me and Jo," and firmly pointed us both in the opposite direction.

Tash muttered darkly all the way to the restaurant. "Don't see why *she* gets to go with them." I didn't, either, to be honest. I thought that probably Auntie Jay reckoned she was giving Ali some kind of treat, not realising that Ali does not regard boys as a treat. Not that I cared; I was too busy brooding over missed opportunities.

I have now had time to think about it and realise that it just goes to show, what they always say in *Glam Girl*: **BE PREPARED**. Ready for that chance meeting which could change your life. For that dream boy that might turn up on the doorstep. In other words, even if you are merely flobbing about at home, you cannot afford to neglect your appearance, for who knows when the door bell might ring and Mr Wonder Guy be standing there on the doorstep? It could happen! They know what they are talking about, those people at *Glam Girl*. As I said to Tash, "We ignore them at our peril."

Well, I have learned my lesson. The whole evening was thoroughly miserable! I just hate hate HATE not looking my best. Tash, of course, had a great time as Orlando was there and she was able to goggle at him, and even brush past him as she made her way to the Ladies. She still hasn't actually spoken to him, but even just feasting her eyes on his divine form is enough – for the moment – to keep her happy. Happy, do I say? *Ecstatic*, more like! She has been going on about it ever since, and I just know she dreams about him in bed.

Auntie Jay was hugely amused. She looked at Tash ogling Orlando, and whispered to me, "Is that the sort of thing you consider hunky?"

I said that we thought he was rather good-looking. "We think he looks like Orlando Bloom."

Auntie Jay said, "Aha! So that's why you wanted to come here?"

I said that it was why Tash had wanted to come. I said that she fancied him like crazy, and Auntie Jay nodded and said, "That explains why she's all got up like the fairy at the top of the Christmas tree!"

I haven't told Tash that this is what Auntie Jay said; it would be unkind. In any case, what does Auntie Jay know? She might be smart and sassy, but she is almost as old as Mum and really has no idea what sort of boys we go for.

We sat at two tables, like this:

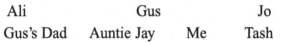

Ali		Gus		Jo
Gus's Dad	Auntie Jay		Me	Tash

It was an absolute total waste, Ali sitting next to Gus; she hardly said a word to him all evening. He hardly said a word to her. Mostly they both just sat in silence. He really *isn't* into girls. I mean, for once Ali was looking quite presentable, so that I wouldn't have been ashamed to tell anyone she was my sister. I felt kind of sorry for her, being so tongue-tied and awkward, and Gus doing nothing whatsoever to help, but they are as bad as each other. If they can't be bothered to make a bit of an effort and just be normally civil – well, quite frankly I wash my hands of them. That is the sort of mood I am in.

I irritably demanded of Ali this morning, as we gloomed about in the aisles of Tesco (Tash still being up on cloud nine and generally out of things), why she hadn't told us that Gus and his Dad were going to be there. Ali, in her vague way, said, "I assumed you knew." She then, *maddeningly*, asked what difference it would have made.

I hissed, "I would have put different clothes on!"

If she had asked me what for, I think I might have screamed and bashed her with a tin of mushrooms; but she just studied me a moment, like trying to work out what the problem was, and said, "I'm going to do frozen stuff this week… pies and stuff. Ready-made meals. Is that OK?"

I said, "Oh, do what you like! What does it matter? I'm sick of food."

Ali said, "Yes, it's such a bore, isn't it? I wish we could just live on pills."

I certainly have no desire to live on pills, as there are too many things that I would miss. Chips, for example. Crisps, for example. Chocolate. Raspberry pavlova. *Doughnuts*. Indian meals, Chinese meals, pizza. I do actually quite like food. Nevertheless it is a great bore having to work out what you are going to be eating every week. Having to go shopping. Having to put stuff away. Having to wash up, having to wipe up. Even just having to open tins. I think I'll be quite glad when Mum is back.

Monday

Something I forgot to mention yesterday (still being in somewhat of a dudgeon about the weekend's disaster):

 Jo is going off to Australia! I cannot help feeling sorry for poor Auntie Jay, left on her own. It's like she's been jilted. I have discussed it with Tash, and we think that she and Jo must have had a lovers' tiff. Well, more than a tiff if Jo is getting out. Looking back on it, they didn't sit together in the restaurant, and I realise now that they didn't really talk all that much – to each other, I mean. Auntie Jay spent most of her time talking to Gus's dad, and Jo talked to me and Tash. It is just so sad. I think I am a big romantic at heart… I want everyone to be in love. I want everyone to be happy!

Tuesday

Still nothing from Wackeen. I am trying very hard to be philosophical, but it is *so* difficult when Tash is going on and on about Orlando all the time. She actually suggested this morning – quite seriously – that instead of staying home and eating Ali's frozen meals we should go into town every day and eat pizzas. Well! I am all in favour of eating pizzas. Unfortunately there is just one small drawback, and that is *money*. We have somewhat overspent even as it is, and I would hate having to go running to Auntie Jay at the last moment to beg for a loan.

I put this to Tash, and she sighed and said, "Yeah, I guess you're right," but I could tell that she was tempted. She is really gone on Orlando! I can sympathise with her, as I know what it is to weave fantasies. I know that a person can become completely obsessed so that it takes over their whole life. But I do just wish she would stop wittering on about him!

Wednesday

Attempting to be chummy, as we came back from school together (Tash having gone racing madly into town to see if Orlando was in the pizza restaurant), I remarked to Ali that I felt so sad for poor Auntie Jay. Ali looked at me in surprise and said, "Why?"

I said, "Being jilted." And then, knowing how clueless Ali is about these things, I added: "By Jo."

Ali said, "Jo isn't *jilting* her."

I thought to myself, oh, dear! Ali is so naïve. I remembered the time when Tash and I were talking about Auntie Jay and Ali went all pinched and quiet.

I didn't want to upset her, I mean I was just looking to have a nice, normal, sisterly chat, not some kind of confrontation, so very quickly I said, "OK, but she's still going off to Australia."

Ali said, "So what?"

I said, "Well, poor Auntie Jay, left on her own."

There was a silence after I said this. I could see Ali's face contorting, like she was on the point of saying something, and then deciding against it, and then nearly saying it, and then not saying it, until finally she burst out with: "Jo's always been going to Australia. That's why she gave up her flat."

I said, "*Oh?*"

Ali said, "Yes, because the lease had run out and she didn't want to renew it."

"So why is she going to Australia?" I said.

Ali said, "Because that's where her boyfriend is."

To say that I was stunned would be to put it mildly. I said, "She's got a *boyfriend*?"

Ali said, "Why shouldn't she have?" She then went on to tell me all about him; how his name was Mark, and he ran a sports centre, and he'd been married before and had two kids, but the kids lived with their mum, who lived in Melbourne, while Mark lived in Perth, "which is right the other side of Australia."

How on earth does she know all this??? It's just another example of Ali never telling us things. She is so secretive! She keeps everything hugged to herself; it's not at all sisterly of her. Somewhat grumpily I said, "Auntie Jay is still going to be left on her own."

"Maybe not for long," said Ali.

I said, "What do you mean, not for long? D'you mean she's found someone else?"

At which Ali immediately went all vague and said, "Maybe. Maybe not. I don't know!"

I don't think, probably, that she does, though with Ali you can never be sure. She has now gone into mysterious mode and refuses to discuss it. Talk about maddening!

When Tash turned up, which she did a bit later, I tried telling her about Jo and her boyfriend and his two kids that live in Melbourne, thinking it would interest her, but all she could talk about was Orlando. She had seen him! She had touched him! They had spoken!

"He's Italian!" *Screeeeech.*

She still doesn't know his name. She still hasn't had a proper conversation with him. Not like I had with Wackeen. She hasn't actually had *any* sort of conversation with him. All that happened, as far as I can make out, is that Tash went prancing into the restaurant, deliberately crashed into him, cried, "Oops, sorry!", *he* cried, "Oops, sorry!" (in an Italian accent), Tash splashed out on one measly little helping of dough balls and came screaming back home on cloud nine, flushed with success, to tell us about it.

She is still telling us about it, two hours later. I'm sure I didn't go on like this about Wackeen! It really seems a bit excessive. Plus I am beginning to think that this guy doesn't actually look like Orlando Bloom at all. There is a picture of the real Orlando in this week's *Glam Girl*, and quite frankly Tash is deluding herself if she reckons her Italian waiter bears any resemblance. The real Orlando is gorgeous. Her one is really rather coarse. He has big red hands and a huge nose and *pimples*. She is welcome to him!

Thursday

Such excitement! We have seen underpants!!! I am tempted to add, "Like it's the first time?" But they were hanging out to dry on the balcony below, a whole little line of them, all different colours, fluttering in the breeze. Really cute! It was Tash who first caught sight of them. She came giggling over, going, "Underpants!" and stuffing her hand into her mouth. Ali looked at her like she was mad. Tash squealed, "Come and see!" so I went, and we leaned out together and speculated which ones belonged to Gus and which ones belonged to his dad. This naturally led to further speculation as to what sort of underpants the divine Orlando would wear. Tash's Orlando, that is; not the real one.

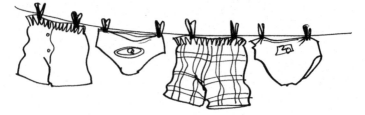

I said, "He probably wears those horrible flappy things."

Tash screeched, "He does not!"

Well! How would she know? She doesn't, of course. Trying to be helpful I rushed to get my latest copy of *Glam Girl*, where there is a double page spread entirely devoted to male under garments. A fascinating subject!

We sat at the table and pored over them, deciding which were the most sexy. I chose some stripy purple ones, Tash went for mock leopard skin. Rather vulgar, and *very brief.* We tried to interest Ali, but she took one look and went, "Ugh! Hairy legs!" I said that Orlando probably had hairy legs, being Italian. Tash, defiantly, said that she liked blokes with hairy legs, at which Ali and I, in chorus, shrieked, "Yeeeurgh!" At least there is something we agree upon.

Shortly after we had done our underpants survey, Tash suddenly, for what seemed like no reason at all, said to me that if I still haven't heard from Wackeen by the end of the week, why don't I try writing to his sister and asking her to forward a letter. I know why she said it. She feels sorry for me! She has Orlando, and I have no one. But as I said, I don't know what his sister's name is. I can hardly just put "Joaquin's Sister" on the envelope. Tash said she didn't see why not, but I told her I am not that desperate. I don't need her feeling sorry for me, thank you very much! I mean, it is nice to know that she cares, and I'm sure that I would feel the same in her place, but considering she doesn't even know what *Orlando's* name is, let alone the name of his sister… I rest my case! And anyway, he is nowhere near as good-looking as I first thought.

But why, why, *why* didn't I get Wackeen's address???

Friday

The most terrible panic. We had just got back from school – me and Tash; I don't know *where* Ali was – when the phone rang. It was me who answered it. I heard Auntie Jay's voice ring out merrily in my ears: "OK, girls! Spot check, five minutes."

I couldn't immediately think what she was talking about. I went, "S-spot check?"

Auntie Jay chirped, "I promised I'd give you due warning."

And then I remembered… way back when we first moved in she threatened us with the odd visit to make sure we weren't trashing the place or turning it into a festering heap of garbage.

I said, "Oh! Yeah, right... spot check. No problem!"

Auntie Jay said that she would be "Up in five."

I slammed the receiver back and reeled away across the room, feeling faint and moaning, "Spot check... Auntie Jay's coming up!"

Tash shrieked, "Not *now*!"

I said, "Yes, now! In five minutes!"

"She can't!" wailed Tash.

But she could, and she was, and as we gazed around us, in a kind of stupefied fashion, I realised that a festering heap just about describes the way we have been living. It's odd, cos you don't notice it until you are suddenly forced to see it through someone else's eyes. What we saw was not pleasant. For starters, there were clothes all over the place. Literally *all over*. Clothes on the sofa, clothes on the chairs, clothes on the floor, clothes on the table... clothes littering the bed, clothes draped over the bathroom door, clothes hanging off the backs of chairs. Muddy trainers on the draining board. Knickers – heaps of them! – in the middle of the floor. Filthy gym kit scrunched up in a corner. A pair of someone's tights, possibly mine, dangling from the lampshade.

There were also: (dirty) dishes in the sink, (dirty) dishes on the draining board, (dirty) dishes on top of the stove, not to mention bedclothes in the bath (the ones

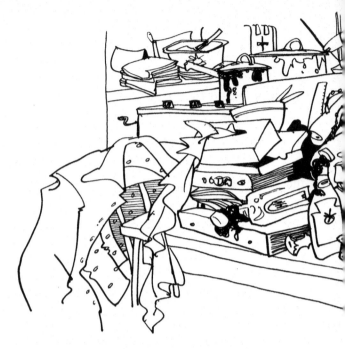

we'd washed but hadn't yet got around to ironing). As for the table – well, quite frankly, you couldn't even see the table for the junk that was cluttered on it. Books, papers, make-up, tissues, old crumpled crisp packets, gungy sauce bottles, jars of marmalade, bits of bread, stale biscuits, toast crumbs, orange peel, apple cores, sweet wrappers... These are just a few of the things I happen to remember. Usually when we sit down to eat – if we do sit down – we've just been clearing a space in the middle. Looking at it now, the way Auntie Jay was going to be looking at it, we could see that in fact the place was a tip.

That was when panic set in. I screeched, "Do something, do something!" and began snatching at the dishes in the sink and frantically piling them into the

cupboard underneath, amongst the cleaning stuff. Tash seized a bin bag and began sweeping all the junk off the table. I went round grabbing clothes and stuffing them haphazardly into drawers. Any drawers! Lots of them went in with the knives and forks. Just so long as they were out of the way. We took the bedclothes out of the bath and crammed them into the bin bag, which we then bundled under the sink. It was all rather disgusting, really; I mean, mixing dirty stuff in with clean stuff, beautiful spotless sheets all scrunched up with orange peel and yucky apple cores, but we simply didn't have time to get it all sorted. This was an emergency!

At the last minute I went to the fridge to put away an open carton of milk that Tash had missed and found that

the freezer bit at the bottom wasn't quite closed – again.
There seemed to be something stopping it, and when I
looked inside I saw what it was: *ice*. Huge great mounds of
it, spreading all over like some kind of creeping crystalline
fungus. Obviously somebody who shall remain nameless
but certainly wasn't me had gone and put stuff in there
without bothering to check that the door was shut properly
and without putting the bucket back in front of it. (I
strongly suspect that it was Tash, though she denies it. But
it is the sort of slapdash thing she is capable of.)

All I could do, with great presence of mind – well, *I*
think it showed great presence of mind – was bash at the
ice with a hammer, knocking enough chunks off it to get
the door closed, in the hope that Auntie Jay wouldn't

want to look inside cos quite honestly it was like something out of the polar regions, a great frozen waste, and I didn't want us getting a bad report. Specially not after Mum went to all that trouble when we moved in, giving us lessons in fridge-door closing.

I'd just slung the hammer back under the sink when there was a knock at the door. Tash, running distractedly about the room with her dirty trainers, squeaked, "Help, help, what shall I do with these?" and flung them in the oven. I clawed up a pair of knickers that had escaped my earlier clothes gathering and stuffed them under a sofa cushion. In the nick of time. Phew!

Auntie Jay was quite impressed. She said, "Well, I congratulate you, you've kept the place really neat and tidy." We had, too! Well, if you didn't look too carefully, which fortunately Auntie Jay didn't. She opened the fridge, but only the top part, not the polar regions, and she just glanced in passing at the sink, which was just as well as we afterwards discovered it was coated in some kind of greasy grey mould. *Not* very wholesome. I did notice that the carpet seemed to have changed colour from what it was when we moved in, and Tash obviously noticed it, too, as she somewhat nervously explained to Auntie Jay that "We haven't actually done the – um – ah – vacuuming yet. We do it like – um, ah—"

"Once a week," I said. (More presence of mind!)

Tash said, "Once a week."

"On a Friday," I said.

"On a Friday," said Tash.

I added helpfully, in case Auntie Jay might not be aware, that Friday hadn't yet finished.

Auntie Jay said, "Quite," and went to look in Ali's little room. We didn't know – at the time – what she saw, as we never go in there, but whatever it was she shut the door on it double quick, saying, "Yes… I think perhaps we'd better draw a veil over that."

Tash, being a bit cheeky, said, "Do we get a gold star for the rest?"

Auntie Jay said, "How about a silver one?" She then told us that she thought we'd done "a really good job these last few weeks" and had proved we were "mature and responsible".

She said, "Your mum and dad will be proud of you."

That made us glow! But after Auntie Jay had gone back downstairs we went to look in Ali's broom cupboard and see for ourselves what it was that had to have a veil drawn over it. Tash cried, "My God, what has she done?" It's like some kind of mad maze. I mean, you can hardly move in there. The bed is *entirely*

hemmed in by stacks of books and videos, and there are great mountains of paper, almost up to the ceiling (which is admittedly quite low). On top of the mountains there are piles of clothes, along with an assortment of cups and plates and glasses – plus Fat Man, beaming down at us. Between the stacks there is this narrow path leading to the bed. It is *so* narrow that if you were a plump sort of person, like Avril, for instance, you would never be able to squeeze your way through. Even Ali probably has to go sideways.

I said, "She is completely loopy."

"Barking mad," said Tash.

I mean, practically certifiable. It is considerably annoying when you think of all the hard work we put in, clearing the rest of the place up. If it hadn't been for Ali and her beastly broom cupboard, we might have had a gold star instead of a mere silver. Trust her!

She arrived just a few minutes after Auntie Jay had left, and we both tore into her. We told her that Auntie Jay had been up, doing a spot check, and that we had had to tidy things away all by ourselves. Tash said, "We got it all looking *really good* – and then she opened your door and nearly freaked!"

I said, "How can you *exist* like that?"

To which Ali had the nerve to retort that it was no worse "in there" than it was "out here".

With some irritation I said that that was not the point. "The point *is,* we did all that clearing up and then she went into your room and she had to draw a veil, it was so gross."

"You can't even *move*," said Tash.

Ali said, "I can."

I don't know what it is with Ali, but she is becoming very *difficult*. It's just started happening, just this last week or two. She will no longer accept any sort of criticism, even when it is for her own good, and she has developed this maddening habit of answering back. She never used to be like this! She has always had a stubborn streak, like she has always insisted on doing her own thing. But she never used to argue and snap all the time. It's like she has suddenly become madly full of herself and won't listen to a word that anyone says. I mean, there wasn't so much as a *hint* of apology for the foul state of her room and the fact that she wasn't here to help tidy up, and when we asked her where she'd been she practically told us that it was none of our business.

I said, "Ali, we're not prying, we're just interested. We'd always tell you where *we've* been." But she still wouldn't say. I can't imagine what she has to be so secretive about as she is the last person to have *assignations* i.e., with Unsuitable People. Tash, giggling, suggested that maybe she had been out with Mr Swetman, who takes us for German and once seduced a girl in the games cupboard. Well, that is the rumour. It probably isn't true, but he certainly looks like someone who would seduce people in games cupboards.

Tash said, "*Have* you? Come on, tell us the truth! You've been in the games cupboard with Mr Swetman, haven't you?"

Normally Ali would fire up, bright red and hot as a chilli pepper, if anyone teased her like that. Today she just snapped, "Oh, for goodness' sake, stop being so childish! I'm going to get something to eat."

 Tash and I looked at each other and pulled faces. We both agree that something very odd is going on.

It is now nearly midnight. We have spent all evening vacuuming and dusting and putting things away. Totally dreary, but it had to be done. We have even scrubbed the sink and ironed the bed stuff. Oh, and we have carted *two bags* full of rubbish down to the bin. Ali has been helping us, but has done nothing whatsoever about the state of her broom cupboard. Well, she did bring out a few dirty plates and glasses, but that is all. We have no idea whether she intends to do anything about the rest of the squalor, and we do not intend to ask. We are sick of domesticity.

Tomorrow – hooray! – it's Shauna's party. The last one of the term. It should be good, I am looking forward to it. She has promised us boys galore!!!

I think I am going to turn the light out now as all this horrible housework has made me really tired. Tash is already snoring happy little pig-like snores at my side. It's so strange to think that this time on Sunday we shall be back home with Mum and Dad and sleeping in our own separate beds. I have grown quite fond of Tash's snoring!

Week 9, Saturday
We have just got back from the party. It was quite a good one, I would probably give it about eight out of ten, but *sadly lacking* in the boy department. If Shauna's idea of boys galore is a couple of weedy cousins and one of their friends, then all I can say is that we have very different standards. I mean, three boys and eight girls! Pur-lease! Especially as two of them were only twelve, and the one that was thirteen looked about eleven.

A bit too young for my taste. I suppose I am quite sophisticated as I really only fancy older men. Wackeen, for instance. He must have been at least fifteen. Tash's Italian waiter is more like seventeen, though I notice she has been rather quiet about him these last couple of days. Still, it was a fun evening, and especially when we sat down at the end to watch a vampire movie which had us all screaming and hiding our heads in our hands. It was really s-s-s-s-scary! I think even the boys were scared, though of course they pretended not to be.

Shauna's dad gave us a lift afterwards. It was really late, almost eleven o'clock, but Auntie Jay had said it would be OK so long as we were brought home. We called out to her that we were back, and she put her head round the door and said, "Did you have a good time?" We assured her that we did.

I said, "We saw this brilliant movie – *Revenge of the Vampires.*"

Auntie Jay said, "Sooner you than me. I hope it doesn't give you nightmares... I'd be really spooked!"

Me and Tash are not in the least bit spooked. We are made of sterner stuff! Fangs dripping with blood don't faze *us*. Not even stakes being driven through hearts, though I must admit it was a bit yucky when one person that got bitten started to jellify, so that his skin kind of, like, bubbled, and his face turned to mush, and both his eyes went melting out of their sockets and slithering and slurping down his cheeks before going *plop* off his chin and lying there on the ground like two puddles of poached egg. That was truly gross!

We crept up the stairs as quiet as could be, hardly even daring to breathe, in case people were asleep. No one can accuse us of being inconsiderate! I guess Ali must be asleep as her door is closed and we can hear no sound of television.

Oh! Tash has just interrupted me to say that in fact Ali isn't here. She says she has looked in her cupboard and it's empty. I have asked her how she could tell. I said that Ali probably *was* in there, but disguised as a newspaper. Rather witty, I thought! But it seems that it is serious; at any rate, Tash is taking it seriously. She says we are not supposed to be out at this time of night, and have I any idea where Ali could be?

The answer is no; I didn't bother asking. I would only have got my head snapped off again, or been told that it was none of my business. She has made it quite plain she thinks we are being nosy. All she would have said was that she had "things to do" or "somewhere to go", so we wouldn't have been any the wiser.

Tash has just come bursting back into the room. She has been downstairs to check the book. Ali hasn't signed out, but she is definitely not in her cupboard. Where on earth can she be? Tash is now ringing Auntie Jay, to see if she is downstairs.

She isn't; Auntie Jay hasn't seen her all evening. Tash says she is coming up, right away. I'm worried, now! Really worried. Ali is *so* absent-minded. And not in the least bit streetwise. She is not safe to be let out! She is too naïve. She'll talk to just anybody. People in doorways, total strangers. It never occurs to her that she might be putting herself in danger.

Oh, God, please let her be all right! Wherever she is, please take care of her. Make her come back! I couldn't bear it if anything happened to Ali!

The Ending

I am not keeping a diary any more; I feel that I've had enough. All this writing, writing, writing. Maybe one day I'll start again, but for the moment I am totally *written out*. This is the last entry I shall make.

Two weeks have passed since the night Ali went missing. I don't think I have ever been so frightened in my life as I was that night. I remember how Auntie Jay came tearing up the stairs. I could tell, immediately, that she was as scared as we were. By then it was gone half-past eleven. Ali had *never* stayed out that late before. She might occasionally have lost track of time, she might have forgotten where she was supposed to be, she had even rung home once to say that she was lost, and could Dad go and get her. But now it seemed like she had just disappeared off the face of the earth.

Auntie Jay wanted to know when we had last seen her. We said that we had left her in the flat when we went off to the party. Auntie Jay said, "And what was she going to do? What were her plans?" We had to explain that we didn't know because we hadn't asked.

Tash said, "We've given up asking, it's useless, she never tells us anything."

I added that we had tried. I didn't want Auntie Jay thinking we had neglected her, or not shown any interest. "She just won't communicate."

Auntie Jay then said something which gave us a bit

of a jolt. She said, "Well, I'm not altogether surprised… you do rather tend to patronise her, don't you?"

I said, "*Us?*"

Tash said, "*Patronise?*"

Auntie Jay said, "Oh, now, come on, you know you do! The only reason the poor girl doesn't tell you things is that she's scared you'll start having a go at her."

I thought, well! So that's all the thanks we get. I was really shaken, though. Tash, very earnestly, said, "It's for her own good. We're only trying to help!"

Auntie Jay said that she wasn't sure Ali needed our help. She said, "Your sister has a mind of her own. She's a very interesting young woman, never underestimate her! We've had some extremely illuminating conversations, she and I. Now, where do you think she can have gone? You must have some idea!"

Considerably chastened, we said that she was probably with Louise. Auntie Jay said, "Then let's find Louise's number and ring her." We had to look it up in the telephone book. While Auntie Jay was dialling the number, me and Tash exchanged glances. I think we were both a bit taken aback by the things Auntie Jay had said. Plus, even though I was by now approaching a state of panic, with my stomach tying itself in knots, I couldn't help feeling just the teeniest tiniest tidge of jealousy at the thought of Ali having all those "illuminating conversations" and Auntie Jay thinking so highly of her.

I was hoping that when she got off the phone she would say that Ali was round at Lou's and had simply forgotten to tell us that she was sleeping over; but she didn't. Instead, very quietly, she said, "The Wagstaffes aren't at that number any more. They moved up to Manchester six weeks ago." I was, like, dumbfounded. Louise had moved and Ali hadn't even bothered to mention it? I said this to Auntie Jay.

I said, "Louise was her best friend! She was her *only* friend! How could she not have told us?"

Auntie Jay said, "That's the question you have to ask yourself. Did you not notice she wasn't in school any more?"

Tash muttered that we weren't in the same class. "She was Year 9."

Auntie Jay said, "Yes, of course, and there are just *so many* of you!"

I think she was being sarcastic as there are only three hundred people in the whole school. And now that she had mentioned it, I realised that somewhere at the back of my mind I *had* been aware Louise wasn't around. We always used to see her and Ali sitting together at lunch,

and hanging out together during break. These last few weeks, Ali had mostly been on her own. It wasn't that we hadn't noticed; we just hadn't bothered to think what it meant.

Tash wailed, "Where can she be if she's not with Louise?" Auntie Jay said that was what we had to find out. She told us to "Come along!" and set off downstairs, with me and Tash trailing after her.

My heart was now beginning to thump quite alarmingly. I had these terrible visions of Ali running away because we had been so mean to her. Patronising her, and being impatient with her. Finding fault with the way she looked, the way she dressed. The way she just *was*. I thought, "Please let her come back safely and I will never criticise her again!"

Downstairs, in Auntie Jay's basement, Mr O'Shaugnessy was slumped on the sofa, gazing bleary-eyed at the television. We were quite surprised to see him there. We were even more surprised when Auntie Jay, very sharply, said, "Andrew, wake up! Get your act together. Where's Gus?"

Gus's dad is a very woolly sort of man. He was

wearing his baggy cardigan again. He struggled to sit up, saying, "Gus?" Like he couldn't quite place who Gus was. He probably has his mind on higher things, being an educational person.

Auntie Jay snapped, "Yes, Gus! Where is he?"

Mr O'Shaugnessy said he supposed he was still upstairs. He said, "He was when I left him."

Auntie Jay said, "By himself? Ali wasn't with him?"

Mr O'Shaugnessy said, "Not as far as I can remember… no, I'm sure she wasn't."

Auntie Jay is not someone who believes in wasting time. She was whizzing back up the basement steps, with me and Tash whizzing behind her, almost before Mr O'Shaugnessy had managed to peel himself off the sofa. I wanted to tell her that it was no use asking Gus where Ali might be as they never had anything to do with each other, and in any

case Gus wasn't into girls; but by now his dad had caught up with us, so I didn't quite like to.

It was Tash who said, "Why should Gus know where Ali's gone?" For some reason Auntie Jay seemed to think he might, but when his dad opened the door and we all trooped inside, the flat was empty.

Auntie Jay said, "Right! Where is he? Come on, Andrew! Where could he have gone?"

Mr O'Shaugnessy scratched his head and said he didn't know. "He didn't mention anything about going anywhere. He would have told me if he were."

Auntie Jay didn't seem to think that was good enough. She said, "Oh, really, Andrew! Where is he *likely* to have gone? You must know some of the places he goes to. *Think!*"

While Mr O'Shaugnessy was thinking, I drifted back out on to the landing. I was sort of half expecting, and half praying, that I would see the front door open and Ali come through it. I don't quite know what it was that made me glance upstairs, to our own landing. I think maybe it must have been Fat Man, chirruping to get my

attention, because when I looked up I saw him, perched on top of a stepladder. I couldn't remember the stepladder being there before, though they must have been there when we came back from the party. But they were pushed to one side, in the shadows, so that I still might not have noticed them if Fat Man hadn't chirruped. I tugged at Auntie Jay's arm and said, "Look! What are they doing there?"

Auntie Jay cried, "The roof!" and went charging up the stairs, two at a time.

Me and Tash had never realised that you could get on to the roof. Just above the steps was a skylight, which Auntie

Jay pushed open. We saw her head disappear, while the rest of her stayed where it was; then a second later she came back down the steps, with this big goofy smile on her face and said, "Sh… go and have a look!" For once I got in ahead of Tash. I was up those steps *so fast*. I don't know what I expected to see, but I would  never have guessed, not in a thousand million years, the sight that greeted me: Ali and Gus, fast asleep in each other's arms, tucked away in the angle of a chimney stack…

Well. I just could hardly believe it. Ali, of all people! And Gus. It seems he is into girls, after all; he's just shy. I guess me and Tash were a bit too much for him. A bit too high-powered. But he and Ali, it's like they were made for each other. It turns out they had been dating for weeks – and Ali had never said a word! It did sort of explain a few of the things which had puzzled us, like Ali buying new clothes and getting all dressed up the night we went to the pizza restaurant, and Auntie Jay hauling Tash out of the car so that Ali could go with Gus. Cos Auntie Jay knew what was going on. She'd known for ages. Me and Tash were the only ones who didn't.

Looking back on it, I have to admit that we really didn't know very much about anything. *We* didn't know, for instance, that Auntie Jay and Gus's dad were an item. Ali did! She even knew that they were thinking of getting married, but because she had been sworn to secrecy she couldn't tell us.

She did tell us what she and Gus were doing on the roof. She had to, cos both Auntie Jay and Gus's dad demanded an explanation. Not that it is particularly dangerous on the roof, as it's totally flat and there is a parapet; but as Auntie Jay sternly informed them (when we had woken them up and got them back down), "We've all been having heart attacks, wondering where you were!"

Apparently they'd spent the evening looking at star stuff on the computer, and then, as soon as it was dark, they'd sneaked up to the roof to peer at the night sky through Ali's telescope. Excitedly, Gus said, "We wanted to see Scorpius. July's one of the months! It's only in July,

August and September that you can actually see the whole constellation."

Can you believe it? He is as bad as Ali! Tash said, "Another astrology freak!"

Together, they both snarled, "*Astronomy!*"

Well, whatever. They are obviously soul mates.

We are so glad for Ali! We like to think we may have helped a *little*, giving her all that advice about clothes, and hair, etc. But mainly, it has to be said, it was the astronomy that did it. Right from the day of our party, when Gus picked up the picture of the red midget, or the red dwarf, whatever it was, they have been having these long, earnest conversations about black holes and nebulas and the Milky Way. And then when Ali got her telescope... well! That was it. Star-gazers united! Saturday wasn't the first time they had been up on the roof, spooning together beneath the night sky, kissing and cuddling as they scanned the galaxy for heavenly bodies. Ali just giggles when we tease her about it. Mum says to lay off, but I don't think Ali really minds.

She and Gus are so cute together! It's really sweet to see them, sitting on the sofa holding hands. And what is specially nice is that me and Tash aren't in the *least* bit jealous. We wondered if we might be, seeing as Gus is practically a heavenly body in himself. He is still the most gorgeous guy that we have ever set eyes on (in real life, that is. I don't count movie stars). But we have discussed it, at some length, and are in total agreement: it is only fair that Ali should have him. After all, she is older than we are. She is also (according to Tash) *nicer* than we are. I don't quite know what she means by that! But we are both really, really happy for her.

We have been back at home now for almost a fortnight. We did enjoy managing on our own, but I must say it is a huge relief not having to bother any more about feeding ourselves and doing the shopping and washing sheets. Next week we break up. Yippee! Peace and quiet for a whole two months! During which time we are hoping that Miss Selby will go away and have a sex change, or turn into a garden gnome, or something.

It is no longer a secret about Auntie Jay and Mr O'Shaugnessy. They are getting married in September! That will be fun, and something to look forward to. Another thing is our birthday, mine and Tash's, in August. We are going to have the best party ever! Dad has promised that he will hire a hall and get a DJ and we

can ask as many of our friends as we like. He says it is
our reward for being "mature and responsible" while he
and Mum were away. We are going to invite absolutely
everyone we can think of, even silly little babies like
Daisy Markham, and this time there really are going to
be BOYS GALORE. Boys by the bucket full!

At least, there are if we can find any. We have already
started looking…

Lightning Source UK Ltd.
Milton Keynes UK
UKOW04n2103061217
314006UK00006B/157/P